SEAL
Next Door

SEALS OF CORONADO

PAIGE TYLER

SEAL
Next Door

PROLOGUE

Indonesia

"ARE YOU SURE WE'RE ON THE RIGHT ISLAND?" Petty Officer 2nd Class Sam Travers of SEAL Team 5 whispered into his mic as he used his night vision goggles to scan the darkened beach below the sand dune where he hid. "Because there's nobody out here. And as far as meeting places go, you've got to admit this place is desolate as hell."

Understatement. He hadn't so much as spotted a bug since he and his Teammates had gotten there.

"I know it doesn't look like much, but this is definitely Kepulauan Nenusa," Holden Lockwood, the SEAL in charge of this mission, announced over the radio—from wherever he was hidden further down the beach. "And if you paid attention during the mission briefing,

2 | PAIGE TYLER

you would have heard the CIA analyst telling us that the players for this meeting are going to wait until the last minute to show up. Both sides seem to distrust the other and neither wants to be the first one here."

Sam grunted a noncommittal response. That part about him not paying attention during the briefing was his Teammate ragging on him because he was still the effing new guy—even if he had been on the team for nearly six months now. Besides, it wasn't like he thought the boat had dropped them on the wrong island. He was more concerned that the analyst Holden mentioned might have had the location wrong to start with. It wouldn't be that surprising, considering this little postage stamp of dirt they were currently hanging around was one of over seventeen thousand islands in this part of the ocean. Would it be so shocking if the CIA had mistakenly sent them to the wrong place?

"Speaking of CIA analysts," his best friend on the Team, Wes Marshal, interrupted. "Is there any chance that he told you who the hell we're supposed to be running surveillance on out here in the middle of nowhere? Because I couldn't help noticing it never came up during the briefing."

"No, they didn't tell me," Holden admitted. "They said it was need-to-know and we didn't need to know. They told me our job was straight recon and surveillance. Find a position to observe the meeting, then get all the photos, videos, and audible recordings we can without being seen."

The other two members of their SEAL Team, Dalton Jennings and Lane Roberts, joined in then with their thoughts about being sent out on a mission with no idea who they might be dealing with.

"If something goes wrong, we won't even know who's shooting at us," Lane pointed out. "Or if we should shoot back."

That cheery announcement was met with more than a few grunts of annoyance over the radio.

"Well, there's nothing we can do about it now," Holden said. "Just make sure your position is as well camouflaged as you can make it. We don't want anyone seeing us if they happen to wander our way."

Since they might be there a while, Sam decided to get comfortable where he was on the backside of the sand dune. Lane joined him a few minutes later.

"I figured I might as well move closer," Lane said, setting down his lightweight video gear, then scraping a shallow foxhole in the sand beside Sam. "That way we can cover each other if this shit goes sideways."

Sam didn't bother calling out his Teammate on his utter BS. Lane moved closer because he wasn't crazy about spending the next three or four hours in silence, listening to the waves and waiting for people who might never show up when he could be talking. Sam supposed he couldn't blame him.

"So, what's the deal with you and Noah's apartment?" Lane asked two minutes later as he checked the image on the night capable camera, then shut it down. "You sign the lease yet?"

Sam realized that Lane's voice hadn't sounded in his earpiece, which meant he'd turned off his mic. Sam did the same to his, knowing Holden wouldn't appreciate the unnecessary chatter over the radio.

The "Noah" in question was Noah Bradley, one of their Teammates. Noah had been lucky enough to stumble into one of those love-at-first-sight kind of relationships with a woman who also happened to be rich as well as beautiful. Or at least richer than a Navy SEAL, which probably wasn't saying much. Regardless, Noah was now living in an awesome beach front house that was one of the nicest places Sam had ever seen. While he was happy his buddy was living it large with an ocean view, the thing that mattered most was that Noah had given up an apartment in a great part of San Diego with an extremely manageable rent and free wi-fi.

"Damn right," Sam said, scanning the surf line for the arrival of their targets. "I was there to sign on the dotted line the second Noah turned in the keys. I even agreed to take the place as-is, no repainting or cleaning necessary. I didn't have time to move in before we got called up for this mission, but at least the apartment is mine."

"Cool," Lane said. "If you need help moving your stuff from the dorms, just ask."

"I don't have much stuff, but I'll take

whatever help I can get. Moving my bed and couch up those stairs would definitely not be fun on my own."

Lane glanced his way in the darkness. "Speaking of being on your own, you got anyone special lined up to help you christen the new place?"

"Nah," Sam admitted. "Truthfully, we've been going on so many missions and training exercises lately, it hasn't been worth it to even try and start something serious with anyone."

His friend snorted. "Who's talking about starting anything serious? Just stop by one of the bars outside the gates of Coronado and pick up the first groupie. Or, better yet, ask Dalton where to go. I know he's married now, but it wasn't that long ago that he was tapping anything that moved."

It was Sam's turn to snort. Having grown up with a dad who used to be a SEAL, he'd learned from his parents that there were plenty of women in San Diego who'd sleep with a guy simply because he *was* a SEAL. Sam personally had nothing against a woman who wanted to do that. *You do you* was his motto for life. But he wasn't interested in any of that for himself. Besides, his mom would have kittens if he ever brought a groupie home to meet the parents.

"No, thanks," he said. "I think I'll wait until I find a girl I'm really interested in before I worry about having them over."

Lane scanned the beach before looking over his shoulder, like he was concerned the bad guys might come at them from that direction, then turned back to Sam. "Looking for the real thing? That's cool. I mean, it isn't the way I'd roll if I were you, but it's your call."

Desperate to get the focus off of him and his love life—or lack thereof—Sam decided to change the subject. "Speaking of women, whatever happened with you and Noah's sister, Laurissa? You guys were supposed to go on a date, weren't you?"

Through his NVGs, Sam saw Lane frown and wondered for a second if he'd hit on a sore subject. Had Lane and Laurissa already broken up before they even got started?

"Laurissa and I have been trying to get together for weeks now," Lane admitted. "But it's like the world is working against us. Every time we plan to meet up, something happens. Either she gets dragged off to do something with her family, or I get sent off on some stupid additional duty tasking from headquarters."

"What kind of additional duties?" Sam asked curiously.

Additional duty crap was a way of life in the military, but SEALs were usually protected from the worst of them because of all the training and deployments they got sent on.

"Crazy stuff," Lane muttered. "Like right before coming out on this mission, Laurissa and I were going to hang out for a couple hours, but then I get a call that I'm needed to help with monthly ammo inspections. A week before that, I had to serve as an honor guard for Captain Hunt at an award ceremony in downtown San Diego. Before that, I got pulled into a late-night accountability check on the Team's night vision goggles. I swear, if I didn't know better, I'd say somebody had it out for me."

Sam opened his mouth to ask who the hell Lane had pissed off—because that seemed to be what was going on—but Holden's voice interrupted him.

"I'm picking up movement in the water. Multiple boats. Everyone get ready."

Sam shoved some more sand around, making extra sure he'd be difficult to spot, then checked the small parabolic microphone resting on the ground in front of him. The thing might be tiny, but from previous use, he knew it'd pick up and record any conversation within two hundred yards.

A few minutes later, five Zodiac-style inflatable boats slid up onto the sand, engines shutting down immediately as twenty or so men in unmarked black tactical gear slipped out and started setting up a perimeter. Seeing the way they moved—along with the folding stock AK-47 variant weapons they carried—made Sam sure they were military of some type, though from where, it was difficult to tell. In this part of the world, they could have been Chinese, North Korean, Cambodian, or even Vietnamese. Though if Sam had to guess, he'd lean toward China or North Korea. Those were the only two countries bold enough to send their people out this far from home.

Sam reached out to flip on the parabolic mic

when several of the men began to head straight toward the dune he and Lane were hiding behind. Sam made himself as small as he possibly could, using his free hand to sweep some sand over the backs of his legs, hoping that'd help hide him.

As two of the men walked up the side of the sand dune, he started to reach for the M4 carbine tucked at his side, but stopped himself. A firefight against these odds wouldn't end well and would completely blow the mission. Instead, he grabbed the mic and stand, tucking it against his chest, resting his face against the sand. Out of the corner of his eye, he saw the men halt halfway up the side of the dune, their backs to Sam and Lane, and he breathed a sigh of relief. But while that was a good thing, it also meant that he and Lane couldn't use the surveillance equipment they had with them, which was the entire reason they were on this beach in the middle of nowhere in the first place.

Just when Sam was about to take a chance and move the mic into position—regardless of the two bad guys standing less than ten feet away—there was a noise from further down the beach. The men in front of him immediately stepped off the dune and moved away, taking up their positions along with their fellow bad guys in a loose semi-circle facing the newcomers.

This group was nearly as large as the first, and as heavily armed. But they definitely weren't military. Based on their mismatched clothing and weapons, they looked like some kind of terrorist group.

Two members of the ragtag group stepped forward to be met by two soldiers from the military team. The four men sized each other up as Sam moved the parabolic mic back up to the top of the dune and turned it on. Words in a foreign language came through the earpiece he had set to listen into the mic, but after a few seconds, he turned it off. There was no reason to listen since he couldn't understand what they were saying. The CIA analysts back at home would go through the memory card and translate everything anyway.

Beside him, Lane was busy taking pictures, focusing most of his attention on the four men in the middle of the circle. Sam didn't blame him. Those four were obviously the ones with the power in this situation. Everyone else was paid muscle.

Sam studied the men, trying to figure out the parts each played in this meeting by the clothing they wore and the way they carried themselves. The two men in the black tactical uniforms were as different as day and night. One was middle height and older while the other was at least six-four and a good ten years younger than the first. He stood silently behind the shorter man, too. The quintessential right-hand man. Just in the extra-large variety.

The two men that Sam assumed to be terrorists were so similar in height and looks that they had to be brothers. Dark-haired, they had beards to match, and both adopted the same aggressive stance as they bartered with the military guy in charge.

And bartering was definitely what was going on, Sam was sure of it. Even without being able to understand anything they said, it was obvious the men were negotiating over something. And whatever it was they were haggling over, it must have been important because the tension down there on the beach was thick enough to choke a goat. Sam half expected someone to start shooting simply so they could all start breathing again.

But nobody shot anyone.

Instead, the military guy handed the terrorists a folder, who gave him a small cloth bundle in exchange. Sam couldn't make out what was in the folder, but it wasn't hard to identify the small glittering gem the soldier took out of the bag. It was a diamond. A big one.

The meeting broke up shortly after that. The two terrorists turned and walked back down the beach in the direction they'd come, one carrying the folder while the other motioned to their men to follow. The military troops stayed exactly where they were, watching them leave.

Then the leader made a motion with his hand and everyone headed for the boats. Everyone except for the big guy. He stood where he was, at first staring down the beach in the direction the terrorists had gone before suddenly turning and looking Sam's way. A split second later, the man started moving purposely toward the dune Sam and Lane were hiding behind.

Sam grabbed his weapon, sure he wasn't

going to have any choice but to start shooting when the man's boss called out from one of the boats they were already sliding back into the surf.

The big man hesitated, scanning the top of the dunes in front of Sam and Lane. Finally, he turned and walked away, wading into the water to catch up to his boat. Once seated, he looked back in their direction, gaze trained on Sam and Lane's position until the boat disappeared into the darkness.

Sam let out a sigh of relief. Beside him, Lane did the same.

"I hope the CIA tells us what that was all about," Sam whispered to Lane as they cleaned up their gear. "Because that was the weirdest crap I've ever seen."

"Hooyah," Lane said.

CHAPTER
One

SAM CURSED AS THE HEAVY STACK OF BOXES IN HIS ARMS shifted, nearly toppling over. He staggered to the left as he reached the second-floor landing, barely keeping the load from falling. Maybe he should have asked Wes and Lane to hang around a little while longer to help with these last few things. They would have stayed, but Sam already felt bad enough about commandeering his friend's Saturday morning. Especially since they'd just gotten back from the mission in Indonesia late yesterday and were all still running on fumes. So, after the guys had helped him move all the heavy stuff—bed, dressers, couch, kitchen table, and TV—he told them to take off, saying he'd get the rest. That was three trips ago. Now, he wished he hadn't been so noble. Even if it was boxes of old clothes, books, and knickknacks that had been sitting in his parents' basement since he joined the Navy, it was still a lot of crap. And it was damn heavy.

He was halfway down the hallway to his new place, trying to balance the stack of boxes in one hand while digging in his pockets for the keys with the other, when a woman came out of the apartment across from his. She immediately turned to check her door, twisting the knob to make sure it was locked, but in those few heartbeats that he'd been able to see her face, he decided she was the most beautiful woman he'd ever set eyes on.

He'd be the first to admit that the word *beautiful* gets tossed around a lot.

It's a *beautiful* day.

Those flowers are *beautiful*.

That dress looks *beautiful* on you.

You have *beautiful* eyes.

It was so overused, it was almost meaningless these days.

But the woman in the hallway wearing shorts, a T-shirt with the name of a local college splashed across the front, and well-worn running shoes, was the true reason the word had been invented in the first place. That's all there was to it. If he looked up *beautiful* in the dictionary, her picture would be right there next to it.

Her long, blond hair was pulled back in a ponytail that swung around in a mesmerizing way as she turned to walk down the hall. He tried hard not to gawk as he got a clear view of her face and plump pink lips, high cheekbones, and alluring hazel eyes. Damn, she could be a supermodel.

Apparently, he failed at the whole not-gawking thing, because one second he was standing there with a stack of heavy boxes precariously balanced against his chest, and the next, they were on the floor, two of them breaking open, letting the stuff inside tumble across the carpet. And he had no idea how it had happened.

He was pretty sure he'd just made a complete fool of himself in front of this goddess of a woman, though.

Maybe she hadn't seen him.

Maybe he could pitch himself down the stairs before she did.

"Oh, no!" a sparkling feminine voice said, confirming she'd seen his clumsy move and that it was far too late to sink into the floor and disappear. "Let me help you with those."

"That's okay," he said, quickly dropping down to one knee to upright the two boxes that had burst open, praying nothing too goofy and embarrassing had fallen out. "I can get it myself."

"Don't be silly," she said with a laugh that had Sam wondering if it was too early to profess his undying love and devotion.

He opened his mouth to stammer out his thanks, but by then, she was already on her hands and knees, scrambling around to pick up some of the stuff that had rolled much further than Sam would have thought possible. The position gave him a perfect view of her perfect butt, perfectly displayed in those little running shorts. Besides the word *perfect*, that kept bouncing around in his head like a rubber ball, all Sam could think was Five Stars! Two Thumbs Up! Thank God for Women!

"Oh, my gosh! You have a Rubik's Cube?"

Her heavenly voice intruded on his moment of worship as she turned around and held up the item in her hand.

As captivating as her butt might be, Sam still

stopped thinking about it when he got a good look at what she was holding up.

"Yeah," he said, a smile tugging at his mouth as he reached out to take the colorful piece of plastic from her. "My dad got it for me when I was a kid."

"From the way you're looking, I'm guessing it brings back some fond memories," she said, her soft voice pulling his attention away from the cube and leaving him to wonder how long he'd been staring at it.

He chuckled, casually tossing the Rubik's Cube up and down in his hand. "I guess it does. My dad traveled a lot when I was a kid, but we would sit for hours playing with it when he got home."

When she didn't say anything, Sam looked up to see her smiling at him. It made her look even more stunning than before.

"What about you?" he asked, handing it to her. "I know these things were before both of our times, but did you ever play with one?"

She laughed again, her hands starting to twist first one side of the Rubik's Cube and then the next, over and over, almost faster than Sam could keep up with. "Oh, definitely. I loved these things when I was a kid. There is no better example of group theory, commutator, conjugation, and disjointed permutations. And it's a wonderful way to explore the development of mathematical algorithms for basic problem solving."

He was so busy attempting to understand what she'd said that he didn't realize she wasn't merely randomly playing with the cube. Not until she handed it back to him, with all six sides completed and a big grin on her face.

"My name is Poppy McCoy, by the way. And if you haven't figured it out already, I love math."

Sam stared at the Rubik's Cube in disbelief. He and his dad had been thrilled when they'd somehow managed to get three sides done.

He flashed her a grin. "Well, Poppy, I'm Sam Travers. And I hope you don't take this the wrong way, but I just discovered that I find brilliant women to be incredibly sexy."

Poppy didn't say anything. Instead, she sat back on her heels, gazing at him with an unreadable expression. Crap, had he pissed her off? But then she laughed.

"You know, coming from anyone else, I think I would have had a problem with that line, but for some reason, coming from you, it seems to work," she said. "So, I'll take the compliment in the way I think you intended it."

"Well, that's good." Grinning, he dropped the Rubik's Cube back in the box. "I was afraid I came off sounding like an idiot."

"Is that an issue for you?" Poppy asked, still smiling as she leaned over to scoop up a bunch of old pictures of him. "Sounding like an idiot, I mean."

He sighed as he straightened up the box closest to him, getting the last few items back into it and closing the lid. "Unfortunately, yes. But I'm working on it. Thanks for pointing it out to me, though."

That earned him another laugh, and Sam chuckled along with her as they finished getting all the stuff back into the second box. He couldn't help noticing that Poppy was taking her time, looking through the last of the photos she'd picked up from the carpet.

"If there are any naked pictures of me in the bathtub when I was in kid, I would like to point out that the water was cold." Getting to his feet, he carried a box over to his apartment and unlocked the door, then glanced at her over his shoulder. "Just so you know, I mean."

Poppy smiled as she tossed the stack of photos into the other box, then picked it up and walked over to join him. "I'll keep that in mind."

"Not that I'm complaining about the help, but I don't want to interrupt your workout," he said, opening the door, then stepping back so she could walk in ahead of him. "Looks like you were about to head out for a run or something."

Poppy shook her head, that beguiling ponytail swinging side to side in a hypnotizing way. But when she caught sight of his dress uniform draped over the back of the couch, she did a double take. She spun around to look at him, her whole body suddenly tense.

"You're in the Navy?" she asked.

"Yeah."

She glanced at the uniform again, then turned back to him. "You aren't a SEAL by any chance, are you?"

Sam had never used his job in the Navy to get girls and he never would. His father had always looked down on that, so it simply wasn't something Sam ever considered. And if admitting it got him a date with the gorgeous goddess in front of him, then he'd be a damn fool not to. Especially since it was true. But he didn't want any woman going out with him because of what he did for a living.

"A SEAL? Nah," he said casually, the lie popping into his head even as he asked himself what the hell he was doing. If he did manage to secure a date with her, she was going to find out what he was. "I'm just a plain old everyday machinist mate."

Luckily, his uniform was face down on the couch, so it wasn't like Poppy could see his SEAL Trident, if she even knew what it was. But he still held his breath as he waited for her to call him out on the fib. Instead, her shoulders relaxed, and she graced him with that smile he was already getting used to.

"Cool," she said. "And don't worry about interrupting my run. Getting in a little strength training before a I head out is good for me."

Sam breathed a quick sigh of relief, still wondering what it was about his uniform, or the idea of him being a SEAL that made her so uncomfortable. "Well, if you're looking for a little high-intensity circuit training, you could always help me carry the last few boxes up from the back of my truck. That way you could get in your lifting *and* cardio at the same time."

Her lips curved as she set the box down on the floor beside the couch. "So, you get help moving it, but what do I get? Besides the workout, I mean."

He chuckled, not sure he'd ever met a woman so quick-witted. He found it incredibly attractive.

"Pizza?" he offered, placing his own box on the floor. "Toppings of your choice. I'll even throw in beer or soda if it helps."

Poppy tilted her head to the side, pursing her perfect lips as she considered that. "Do I have to eat it here with you or can I take it back to my apartment?"

Sam grinned. "Sorry. One time offer. Must be present to win. Offer not valid in Hawaii or Alaska, cannot be redeemed for cash or combined with future offers."

She laughed. "You're on."

He couldn't describe how happy that made him.

"Pineapple or pepperoni?" he asked, pulling his cell out of his pocket.

"Plain cheese," she said. "It's my favorite. And

I have beer and soda at my place...unless that violates the rules of your offer?"

He hit speed dial for the nearest pizza delivery place and put the phone to his ear. "I'm pretty sure there's some wiggle room in the rules when it comes to getting something to drink at your place. Hell, you might even be able to convince me to stay there to eat, if you're persuasive."

"I think I can do that," Poppy said with a smile as she walked out the door and down the hall, leaving Sam struggling to give the pizza place the order as her amazing butt bounced delightfully ahead of him. It was enough to make him completely forget about whatever deal she seemed to have with guys being in the SEALs.

CHAPTER
Two

P OPPY WALKED DOWN THE HALLWAY OF THE SCHOOL'S physics and math building, waving good morning to the handful of students she knew out of the dozens she passed. Considering how few classes she taught, it wasn't surprising she didn't know more of them. But on paper, at least, she was a physics professor at San Diego Mesa College, even if she made a lot more money than one.

Of course, if anyone followed her past the tiny generic office with her name on the door to the unmarked metal door at the end of the corridor, they'd see the expensive key card reader mounted off to one side of the frame and wonder what kind of professor worked behind a secure vault door. Nobody would ever guess she wasn't really a professor at all, but instead worked for a government organization. The super-secret facility was known as the San Diego Project, but she and her colleagues preferred to call it *The Cave*, which was much more appropriate considering the place didn't have a single window. Which, when she thought about it, sucked.

The Cave was loosely associated with Lawrence Livermore National Laboratory, but only in regard to the focus on nuclear weapons. Beyond that, the two organizations had drastically different missions. Lawrence Livermore focused on the U.S. stockpile while Poppy and her coworkers worried about everyone else's. And with all the countries out there that had nukes, it was a full-time job.

Glancing over her shoulder to make sure no one was watching, she slid her ID card across the face of the reader. There was a metallic click, then a buzz as the door unlocked. Once she got inside, she closed it securely behind her.

"Morning, Doc McCoy."

Poppy smiled at the security guard's warm greeting. For someone so big, Roy Booth had one of the softest voices she'd ever heard. "Good morning, Roy."

Behind the desk, Roy sat back in his chair,

swiveling back and forth ever so slightly. "You're rather chipper this morning."

Only Roy would use the word *chipper*. It was one of the things that made him so endearing.

Since she was, in fact, *chipper*, Poppy didn't bother to deny it. Besides, Roy had a whole bank of monitors tucked away beneath the countertop that shielded the front of his desk, and she knew from experience that he watched everyone who approached the building. If he said she looked *chipper* this morning, then it was almost certainly true.

Poppy hadn't thought it would be so obvious, but in her defense, she had a good reason. One who stood a little over six feet tall and had a face that could make a woman forget herself.

"You met someone, didn't you?" Roy pressed, a huge smile crossing his face as Poppy moved over to the door near his desk and placed her hand against the biometric scanner there. "Someone who's not a total jerk, am I right?"

"I'm not telling you anything about my social life one way or the other, Roy," Poppy said with a laugh as she opened the door. "Everyone knows you're one of the worst gossips in the building," she added as it swung closed after her.

"Gossip? What gossip?" a light, feminine voice asked.

Poppy looked over to see Nyla Higgins standing there holding two mugs of coffee. Tall and willowy, her dark eyes were filled with excitement. "Don't tell me you went on a date last night without telling me? You're not allowed to do that."

Grinning, Poppy gratefully took one of the creamy coffee-filled mugs, eager to inhale her dose of morning caffeine. There was no way she'd get out of telling her friend everything that had happened last night. There weren't many women working in *The Cave*, and she and Nyla had become best friends since Poppy's first day there. Nyla was a hopeless romantic and endlessly obsessed with getting Poppy into a long-term relationship. If there was even a small possibility that Poppy had met someone, her BFF would keep digging until she unearthed every tidbit of information.

"It wasn't a date," Poppy admitted, sipping her coffee and heading in the direction of her office, only for Nyla to grab her arm and turn her toward one of the classified briefing rooms. Okay. Obviously, there was something her friend wanted her to see.

"But Roy was right. You *did* meet someone, didn't you?" Nyla pressed as they slipped into the conference room.

Poppy grabbed a seat near the stack of folders on the table, but ignored them for the moment. There'd be no work for either of them until she filled her friend in on all the details.

"I met a guy moving into the apartment across the hall from mine," she said, choosing her words carefully. Not because she wanted to hide anything, but because she didn't want to jinx anything with Sam. "I helped him carry up some of his stuff and we ended up getting pizza afterward. And before you ask, yes, we hit it off."

"Excellent!" Nyla beamed, dark eyes dancing as she slipped into the chair beside Poppy. "Tell me everything about him. What's his name? What's he like? Is he cute? Are you two going out on a date?"

Poppy couldn't help but laugh. "I know you're excited, but slow down a little. I'll tell you all the juicy details. Not that there are many."

"You let me decide that," Nyla said, gesturing with her coffee mug before taking a sip. "Now, spill! And don't leave anything out."

Grinning, Poppy told her friend about

stepping out of her apartment to go for a jog and seeing this absolute Adonis trying to hold up a stack of boxes at the same time he dug around in his pocket for his keys. "He ended up dropping them and some of his stuff went flying. I think it might have been because he was checking me out."

Nyla oohed and aahed over that, sounding more like a teenager than a fellow nuclear engineer. "Adonis, huh? That sounds promising. Tell me about him! What's he like?"

Poppy smiled as she thought of the handsome sailor she'd met the previous evening. "Sam's amazing. And different than any guy I've ever met. I mean, he's gorgeous as sin, but I swear, I don't think he even has a clue how hot he is. He's quick on his toes and clever, but completely grounded at the same time. It was like we've known each other for months instead of just meeting last night. We ended spending hours discussing toppings on pizza and our favorite TV shows, and I wasn't bored for a second. If we both didn't have to get up early for work this morning, we probably would have stayed up half the night."

Nyla grinned so big Poppy thought her friend might pull a face muscle. "So, does this Sam of yours have a job? If he's as hot as you say, I'm thinking stripper is a real possibility."

Poppy almost snorted coffee out of her nose. "No. He's not a stripper...promise." Although, she'd be lying if she didn't say she hadn't been seriously wondering what Sam's body looked like under that tee and jeans he'd been wearing last night. "Actually, he's in the Navy."

The smile faded from her friend's face, a serious expression taking its place. "I thought you'd sworn off Navy guys after that last one. In fact, I clearly remember you saying you'd rather date an unemployed zombie biker before going out with another sailor."

Poppy winced, because she *had* said that. It wasn't that she had anything against zombie bikers, but at the time she'd been reaching for a good analogy and that had been the first thing to come to mind.

"I probably shouldn't have been so extreme," she admitted. "The guy I had a problem with was a SEAL, so it was stupid to exclude everyone in the Navy. Especially here in San Diego, where you can't throw a ball without it bouncing off someone in a blue uniform. Sam's not like that other guy and he definitely isn't a SEAL, so I think he's worth taking a chance on."

Her friend didn't look so sure. Poppy completely understood why. Nyla had been there when Poppy had gotten involved with that stupid SEAL in the first place. They'd been arguing about what men looked for in a woman and Poppy had said something about how men only wanted a bimbo with all looks and no brains. A silly bet was made and the next thing Poppy knew, she was sleeping with a SEAL who had no idea who she really was. It had started as a joke and ended abruptly when Poppy realized she'd be stuck playing a role forever. Not that she'd wanted it to work. There'd been nothing between them except physical attraction. But still, finding out she was right and that he was more interested in her boobs than her brains had been depressing as hell. Enough that she'd swore off anyone in a Navy uniform.

"Like I said, Sam is different." Poppy sipped her coffee. "Hell, we initially bonded over the mathematical properties of a Rubik's Cube. He's not bothered or intimidated by the fact that I'm smart. If he was, he wouldn't have asked me out on a date."

Nyla did a little happy dance right there in her chair, her dark, wavy hair bouncing. "Yes! And honey, if a guy can appreciate a woman who's both beautiful and intelligent, then he isn't just different—he's special."

Poppy smiled. "You're right. Sam *is* definitely special."

Nyla reached out and picked up a thick folder off the stack on the table in front of them and handed it to Poppy. "Well, now that we have the important stuff out of the way, I suppose we should get to work."

Opening the folder, Poppy took out the handful of the eight by ten matte photos inside, then spread them out on the table in front of her. The pics had been taken at long range with a telephoto lens in a low-light setting. The camera must have been insanely good, because even with the dim surroundings, she was able to make out most of the details. Not that it helped. She turned the pictures this way and that, trying to figure out what she was looking at.

"Okay, I'll play along," Poppy said, flipping from picture to picture a few more times before reaching for the next folder and finding more of the same. "What am I looking at?"

"You tell me," Nyla said. "All I can confirm is that these pictures were taken by a covert DOD team a few nights ago somewhere in the Indonesian Archipelago. Two heavily armed groups met on the beach in what's being described as an initial negotiation. One group offered the technical drawings while the other brought a pouch containing one or more cut and polished diamonds."

"Heavily armed groups?" Poppy mused, now looking up from the second group of pictures that looked very similar to the first. "I assume you're talking about terrorists?"

"Probably," Nyla admitted. "Though it's not out of the question that the group offering the drawings had state backing. What state? I have no idea. That's where you come in. What the hell are in these drawings?"

As Poppy spread the photos out on the big conference room table, she realized that some of them were multiple pictures taken of the same section of drawing, each from slightly different angles and at various exposure settings. She picked out the best view of each section of the drawing, discarding the rest, then she started organizing the photos on the table, putting them together like a big jigsaw puzzle. It didn't take long to figure out what she was looking at once she had the pieces lined up right.

"It's a nuclear warhead," she said. "More precisely, a North Korean warhead. Or the detailed technical plans for one anyway. Right down to the warhead serial number."

Nyla groaned. "I was worried you were going to say something like that." Sighing, she got to her feet. "While you keep going through the pictures, I'm going to tell our boss that it looks like someone is trying to sell a nuclear weapon to a bunch of terrorists. I have no doubt they'll be thrilled."

Poppy gave her a frown. "You don't think these terrorists would actually nuke somebody if they get their hands on this thing, do you?"

"I can't imagine why you'd buy one if you weren't going to use it," Nyla said. "Luckily, it's not our job to figure out how to stop something like this. We simply evaluate the threat and tell them if this thing will work."

On that cheery note, Nyla left to tell the

powers that be, leaving Poppy alone with the photos and the job of figuring out if they were actually the plans for a functional nuclear weapon or an elaborate fake. But she didn't mind. Nuclear weapons—especially foreign nuclear weapons—were her specialty.

It was almost enough to make her laugh. All those years in college, taking math, physics, and engineering courses, only to become an expert on foreign nukes working for an organization with no name, never being able to tell a soul outside the walls of *The Cave*.

Not that anyone would have believed it if she told them. As far as the world was concerned, Poppy was simply a college professor.

CHAPTER
Three

"I THOUGHT WE WERE GOING TO HAVE DINNER," POPPY said curiously as Sam pulled his pickup off Hill Street and started south along the narrow boulevard that ran above the cliffs overlooking the ocean.

Sam glanced over at Poppy beside him in the passenger seat. He thought she'd been devastatingly beautiful last night when she'd been casually dressed to go jogging. But now, wearing a yellow off-the-shoulder sun dress and just the slightest bit of makeup, she was so stunning it was hard to keep his eyes on the road.

Which could be dangerous considering it was about a fifty-foot drop to the beach if he suddenly veered too far to the right.

"We're going to dinner, but I thought we'd

do something a little different," he said, turning into a parking lot near the corner of Sunset Cliffs Boulevard and Ladera Street. "You up for a little adventure?"

Poppy expression was curious even as she nodded. "Always."

Grinning, Sam hopped out of the truck and walked around to open her door, offering her a hand as she slipped out. The hem of her sun dress rode up a little as she slid off the seat, exposing a length of long, toned thigh, but he forced himself to keep his eyes locked on her smile, refusing to be *that* guy.

Poppy was quiet as he led her along the walkways that meandered through the Sunset Cliffs Natural Park, but he could tell she wanted to ask what they were doing there. He only prayed his plan for the evening worked out right. He wanted to impress her, but with less than twelve hours' notice, he hadn't had a lot of time to come up with something.

When they walked around the corner in the walkway and came out onto a grassy bluff overlooking the ocean dotted with surfers, Sam heard Poppy gasp.

Maybe he'd pulled this off after all.

As Poppy stood there beaming, Sam wondered what part of the scene she liked more—the visual of the sun slowly sinking toward the blue horizon or the charming little table full of picnic food. But either way, the look on her face told him he'd hit the ball out of the park.

As he guided her over to the small table set on the colorful beach blanket surrounded by throw pillows, he took in the trays of meat, cheese, and fresh fruit, as well as the covered tray of bite-sized pieces of cheesecake and brownies.

The red-haired woman waiting for them smiled. "You're right on time! We just finished setting up your picnic and the sun won't be going down for about an hour, so you two will have plenty of time to talk. Enjoy!"

Before Sam had a chance to thank the woman from the picnic company, she and her assistant were off, both smiling at the look on Poppy's face. They probably got that a lot. When it came to romantic gestures, picnics on a cliff overlooking the ocean had to be at the top of the list.

Poppy looked at him, her face incredulous. "How did you set all this up so fast? Not that I'm complaining, of course, but you know you didn't have to do anything this expensive for a first date, right?"

Sam tried to figure out if he should take a seat across from her so he could look at her, or beside her so they could both have a view of the ocean. The decision was ultimately taken out of his hands when Poppy sat down facing the water and immediately motioned for him to sit beside her.

"I know, but I wanted to do something special—and different," he said as he joined her. "The picnic company handled everything, including the permit to set up in the park, and it wasn't all that expensive. Even if it was, I still would have done it. You're worth it."

The smile Poppy gave him made Sam want to pump his fist in the air and shout *SCORE!* but he controlled himself. He had to keep his cool, calm exterior. So instead, he flipped open the cooler beside him and took out the small cans of flavored sparkling water. He didn't normally drink the stuff, but that's what came with the meal, so he'd make do.

"To first dates," he said after filling the fancy

copper cups and offering his up in a toast. "And hopefully many more to come."

She clinked her cup against his, then took a sip. Sam wasn't sure how long he sat there mesmerized by her beautiful pursed lips before he forced himself to take a drink.

"How was work today?" she asked as they added meat, cheese, fruit, and crackers to their wooden plates. "You mentioned last night that you had to be in stupid-early this morning."

Sam chuckled at the memory, wishing he hadn't needed to say those words because he'd wanted more than anything to spend time with her. But unfortunately, duty really *had* been calling.

"It wasn't too bad," he said. "They had us in early for PT—physical training—followed by hours of equipment maintenance and cleaning. That's what you do in the Navy when the people in charge don't have anything better for you to do. Even with the gloves I was wearing, it still took forever to get the smell of solvent out of my skin."

Of course, Sam didn't mention that the reason they had nothing to do was because they were all waiting around to hear about the outcome of that surveillance op in Indonesia. It had been days since that mission and there hadn't been a peep out of the CIA. In theory, they were supposed to get a briefing about it tomorrow morning, but he'd believe that when it happened.

Sam also didn't tell her that the equipment he and his Teammates spent the day cleaning were carbines and submachine guns. That would have tipped Poppy off that he was something much different than a machinist mate. He hated lying, but he'd created this fake role and now he had to play it—or lose any chance with Poppy.

"How about you?" he asked, biting into some kind of spicy meat that he couldn't name, but still liked all the same. "What's the day-to-day life of a math professor at San Diego Mesa College like?"

Poppy had mentioned where she worked last night over pizza, along with a few details on her teaching credentials. He'd been fascinated to hear that she had her doctorate, but at that moment she seemed surprised he remembered where she taught.

"What?" He grinned. "You didn't think I'd remember?"

She shrugged, nibbling on a piece of cheese. "Actually, yeah. Most of the guys I've dated weren't particularly interested in what I taught, much less where. But to answer your question, today was pretty standard. I didn't have any classes to teach, but did look over a few papers. The rest of the time I was buried in a research project I'm involved in. It was interesting, but dry."

At they ate, they chatted for a while about their respective days. Sam got the feeling that teaching was a relatively small part of what she did on a regular basis. He guessed that came with the doctorate degree. He'd heard professors at that level had to constantly do research and publish papers to maintain their standing in their field.

"There was something you mentioned last night that got me thinking," he said. "About your doctorate degree. Please don't think I'm trying to call you out or anything, but doesn't it take a long time to get a PhD? I mean, you look like you're about my age. Aren't most people close to thirty by the time they get to where you are?"

Poppy froze, the cup of flavored water halfway to her mouth, turning to look at him. For a moment, he thought for sure he'd insulted her or something, but then her shoulders relaxed.

"Do you know that you're the first and only

guy who has ever asked me that?" she said softly. "The first guy to ever make the connection and add up the numbers in your head. I'm not sure if that says more about you or the men I've been dating."

There might have been some question marks in that little diatribe, but something told him that Poppy didn't expect an answer. So instead, he sat there and waited. He'd learned that from his dad.

"When women want your opinion, they'll ask for it. Until then, keep your thoughts to yourself."

"I was always insanely good at math and science," she continued. "Even when I was a little kid. I have no idea why. My parents aren't academics. Dad is an auto mechanic and Mom is a loan specialist at a mortgage company. The most I can say is that they always encouraged me to read. And when I started showing an interest in advanced studies at school, they urged me to pursue them."

"When you say *a little kid*, how old are we talking about?" Sam asked. "Twelve, thirteen?"

She laughed, eating a big lush strawberry, the juice staining her lips an even darker pink than they already were. "I finished high school before I turned sixteen, had my bachelor's from UC

Berkeley by nineteen, and a PhD before I turned twenty-three. So, yeah, I started young."

Whoa.

Sam ate a little more cheese, then a few olives and grapes, thinking about what she'd told him. Poppy must have taken his silence for something different than what it was, because she stopped eating to regard him with an expression halfway between disappointed and accepting.

"It's really not that big of a deal," Poppy said, and he got the feeling she was sorry she'd ever mentioned anything about her education. "I have a couple degrees. There's nothing special about that."

Before his eyes, Poppy was almost shrinking in on herself, her shoulders sagging, gaze trained on the small table, like she was ashamed of what she'd accomplished and how smart she was. Had the other men she'd dated made her feel that way?

"It seems pretty special to me," he said, slipping his fingers under her chin and gently turning her face his way. "In fact, it's impressive as hell. And you should never let anyone tell you any different. I can't imagine how difficult it must have been going to college when you were so much younger than everyone else there. I don't think I would have been able to do it myself."

The expression on Poppy's face was so full of hope and gratitude that it was like watching the sun come up. "Thanks," she said. "Nobody's ever said anything like that to me or even took the time to consider the situation from my perspective."

Sam picked up a strawberry and held it up to her lips. "Well, most people are stupid. So, there's that."

She laughed and bit into the piece of fruit, a little dribble of juice running across her bottom lip and down her chin. She quickly wiped it away with her finger, giving him an embarrassed smile. Damn, he wanted to kiss her so badly right now.

But he didn't want to rush this thing with her. She was too special for that.

As the sun crept closer to the horizon, Poppy told him about reading college texts on math and science while eating lunch in middle school and living at home with her parents during her bachelor's program while her college classmates lived in the dorms or apartments off campus.

"Don't get me wrong. It isn't like I was socially awkward or anything like that guy from *The Big*

Bang Theory," Poppy said when Sam asked about making friends with people older than her. "But when you're under the legal drinking age for the majority of your university experience and are smarter than people in your class older than you are, it can be difficult to connect with people."

"I can see that," he said. "Did you get to party at least a little bit in college, or did you spend all of your time studying?"

"I dated some, but not until I was pursuing my doctorate," she said. "It wasn't difficult finding guys who'd ask me out since the program I was in was mostly made up of men, but I never clicked with any of them."

He grinned. "Well, their loss is my gain."

She blushed, the color rivaling that of the sunset. Both were equally mesmerizing. Sam had lived in San Diego his entire live and would never get tired of the ocean views, but sharing it with Poppy made it feel like he was experiencing it for the first time all over again.

It was almost completely dark by the time the people from the picnic place arrived to clean up. Sam thanked them again and gave them a big tip, saying he and Poppy had a wonderful time.

"Dinner was perfect," she said as they walked to his pickup.

"I'm glad you liked it." Sam grinned, mentally patting himself on the back. "I thought we might do something else, too, if you're up for it."

She flashed him a smile so bright that it lit up the early evening darkness. "Definitely. What do you have in mind?"

Sam's steps were perfectly in sync with Poppy's as they walked up to the second floor of their apartment building. He had one arm draped across her shoulders and she had one of hers wrapped tightly around his waist. She'd been huddled close like that since the middle of the haunted ghost tour they'd gone on after dinner. He wasn't sure if Poppy had truly been scared by all the spooky stories their guide told, but he preferred to think she was using it as an excuse to get close to him.

"I can't believe I've lived here my entire life and have never done a ghost tour," she said when they reached her door. "That was incredible! Though if I come banging on your door in the middle of the night because I can't sleep, you have no one to blame but yourself."

He chuckled as Poppy unlocked the door and led him inside. "I've available for late night support anytime you need me, which makes having me right across the hallway very convenient."

They'd spent the drive home talking about the combination bus and walking tour through several of the coolest places in the city, including Old Town, Sherman Heights, the Gaslamp District, and the El Campo Santo Cemetery. They hadn't seen any ghosts, of course, but the tour guide had been excellent and they'd had a blast. Besides, anything that got Poppy to stick that close to him was a win in Sam's book.

"I had an amazing evening," Poppy said, closing the door and turning in his arms, her body pressed tightly to his chest. "Best. Date. Ever."

Instead of answering, Sam lowered his head and captured her mouth with his. It had been a completely spontaneous decision, but the moment their lips met, he knew he'd never be able to regret it. Incredibly, Poppy still tasted of strawberries. Then again, maybe that was always what she tasted like. Either way, as her lips parted to allow him to tease his tongue into her mouth, he knew he'd never taste anything as intoxicating again.

He didn't realize he'd buried his hands in her hair until his fingers gently twisted into the long strands. Moans rippled from Poppy's throat as he tugged her closer, kissing her harder. She nipped at the tip of his tongue in return, her way of letting him know she enjoyed everything he was doing.

The feel of her firm breasts pressing against his chest made him go hard in his jeans and it took everything in him to stop himself from backing her up against the door and kissing her until she gasped for air.

Sam broke the kiss slowly, lifting his head to see her standing there with a dazed but clearly pleased expression on her face. The look was adorably sexy on her.

"Is there a problem?" she asked, her voice low and silky.

If his cock hadn't been hard before, it sure as hell was now. A fact that Poppy was obviously aware of if the way she was pressing against him was any indication.

"No problem." He gave her another kiss, keeping it semi-PG this time as he tried to keep things under control. "Tonight was beyond perfect, but it's getting late, and while I don't know about you, I have to be up early again tomorrow."

"On a Saturday?" Poppy frowned. "That sucks."

"True," he agreed. "But I was hoping we could pick back up with this tomorrow night after another date. I don't have to work on Sunday."

"I'm completely up for another date tomorrow night." She gave him a sultry smile, grinding against him a little. "Speaking of being up for something, I wouldn't be averse to you sleeping here tonight."

Sam rested his forehead against hers with a groan. He should be in line for a sainthood after resisting this kind of temptation. "The offer is inviting, but this thing we have going is good enough to take our time with, and I have no doubt that if I stay here tonight, sleeping is the last thing we'll be doing."

Poppy seemed to consider his words for a moment, like she was solving some kind of mathematical equation. Which, considering Poppy, maybe she was. He hated that her previous experiences with guys seemed to put her in a place where she had to carefully examine everything a man said to see if he was rejecting her. The thought that she might ever consider him doing that made him want to say the hell with it and that he'd sleep here tonight if it made her happier.

But then Poppy was smiling again as she went up on tiptoe to kiss him almost chastely on the lips. "You know, I've never once had a guy tell me he wanted to take it slow before. It's a new experience, but I think I like it."

Turning, she opened the door, then kissed him again. "I'm looking forward to whatever you have in mind for our next date, but don't think for a second that I'm letting you get out of here so easily tomorrow night."

He slid a hand in her hair again, his fingers tightening possessively. "Don't worry. I like taking my time, but that doesn't mean I'm slow."

After another kiss, Sam was out the door and across the hallway, half thrilled he'd successfully held himself in check and half sure he was an idiot for wasting the opportunity. One look back at Poppy standing there gazing at him with a look of pure heat, had him leaning toward the latter.

CHAPTER

"IF SHE'S SO SMART, WHY IS SHE DATING YOU?"
Dalton asked in his patented southern
drawl.

Sam leaned back in his chair at the conference room table and shook his head. The moment
he'd brought up last night's date, he knew it had
been a mistake. But in his defense, he and his
Teammates had been waiting in the conference
room for over an hour for the after-action briefing on the Indonesian mission. What else was he
supposed to talk about? And yeah, to a certain degree, he supposed he'd wanted to brag a little about
landing a date with a woman as beautiful and intelligent as Poppy. But when the guys had ragged
on him immediately, he realized he'd made a mistake. Dalton's most recent moronic comment had

only confirmed it. Fortunately, Sam hadn't told them her unique name or they probably would have ragged on that, too.

Wes and Lane were mostly interested in where Sam had met her, while Dalton spent all his time trying to pin Sam down on whether there was any video evidence to confirm the existence of his so-called girlfriend. Sam was glad he'd refused to provide any details or Dalton would be looking her up on Facebook right now.

From where he sat at the far end of the table scrolling through something on his phone, Holden ignored the whole conversation—or at least refused to take part in it. Sam was grateful for that at least.

"What does this new girlfriend of yours do for a living?" Lane asked, this time actually acting like he was honestly curious, and not attempting to set Sam up for more ribbing.

"She's a math professor at San Diego Mesa College," he said. "She went to UC Berkley for her Bachelors, Masters, and PhD."

His buddies all went still at that announcement. Even Holden looked up from his cell, a stunned expression on his face.

"A PhD?" Holden repeated. "Exactly how old is this woman you're dating? Not that there's anything at all wrong with dating an older woman, but how much older than you are we talking here?"

Sam's first instinct was to tell Holden to shove it sideways, but he bit his tongue. He'd been a little confused about Poppy's age and the whole doctorate thing, too. His friends had no idea Poppy had skipped so many grades in school.

"She turned twenty-four in June," he said. "When I said she was brilliant, I wasn't kidding. She started college when she was sixteen and got her PhD before she was twenty-three. So, sorry to disappoint you, but I'm not dating an *older woman*. She's my age."

That answer seemed to satisfy everyone except Dalton, who clearly wanted to send more sarcasm his way. But just as the idiot opened his mouth to say something guaranteed to piss Sam off, the door of the conference room opened and Agent Keith Lucero, the CIA analyst who'd originally briefed them on the Indonesian mission, walked in. They'd worked with Lucero a couple months ago on that armed drone thing in Nigeria, so Sam and the other SEALs trusted him. Two other people in suits who had to be CIA agents, too, followed.

Before Sam could wonder why these new agents were at what had been described as nothing more than a simple after-action briefing, Chasen Ward, Noah Bradley, and Nash Cantrell—three of the most experienced members of their SEAL Team platoon—stepped into the room and grabbed seats at the table.

SEALs were usually assigned to missions based on the presumed level of threat, with four of them being used for most operations. The fact that five of them had been sent to that island a few days ago indicated there was something else going on, either in terms of the danger the Team faced or the consequence of them failing. Now, three more of his Teammates were involved, and all Sam could think was that the mission had gotten a lot more serious.

"I didn't know we'd be seeing you on this op, Chief," Holden said, regarding Chasen curiously while two of the CIA agents pulled up a file on the classified computer at the front of the room.

"I didn't either," Chasen said. "Commander

Hunt called thirty minutes ago and told us to get over here for the briefing."

"I guess that's my cue," Lucero added, motioning toward the large wall-mounted monitor now displaying a classified warning screen with the words, *TOP SECRET...SPECIAL ACCESS PROGRAM...PROTECTED INTELLIGENCE SOURCES.* "Bottom line, the CIA has re-prioritized the Indonesian threat, based on the intel your Team collected, Holden. The situation is now considered to present a grave threat to national security and is much worse than anything we imagined when we first sent your team to that island."

Lucero picked up a remote and flipped through the slides until he reached a photo of two men. Both dark haired with beards to match, they were standing on a crowded city street talking to each other. Even though they weren't dressed in military garb, Sam recognized them as the men they'd seen on the island who were in charge of the group they'd pegged as terrorists.

"Meet Abyasa Alatas and his brother, Adika," Lucero said, motioning to each of the men as he said the names—not that Sam was likely to remember which was which because they looked too damn much alike. "They got their start as terrorists kidnapping tourists to fund various bombing attacks throughout the Indonesian Islands. But over time, they've become less focused on the typical terrorist goals and more interested in simply making money. Still, this most recent meeting changes everything."

The image on the monitor changed to a man in his late-forties or early-fifties with sharp features, a fierce gaze, and dark hair starting to show touches of gray here and there. He was wearing a military uniform, and Sam knew without a doubt that he was the guy who'd led the more organized group on the island that night.

"This is Colonel Chung-Hee Kam of the Korean People's Army Strategic Rocket Force," Lucero said. "For the past fifteen years, he's been a major figure in the North Korean long-range missile program, including the development of their nuclear capabilities."

Sam got a sinking sensation in the pit of his stomach. He prayed he was wrong, but with Chasen and their other two Teammates abruptly added to the mission, he couldn't help but think that this was heading in a bad direction.

"And this," Lucero continued, pulling up a picture of a younger man that Sam recognized as the bigger guy who'd stood behind Kam the entire time, silent and looking menacing, "is Kam's right-hand man, Major Kang-Dae Tae. He's been in charge of security at several nuclear weapon storage sites, including Yongdoktong, located near Kusong. He's also known as the person who makes problems disappear for his boss and he's extremely good at his job. Most of the intelligence agencies in the world have attempted to slip into Yongdoktong at one time or another over the years, interested in getting a look at the status of their weapon technology, but no one—not even the CIA, I'm sorry to say—has come close thanks to Major Tae and his security forces. It's not an exaggeration to say the man is responsible for the death of at least twenty covert agents over the past decade or so."

"What the hell are two men like that doing on an Indonesian island in the middle of the night with people like the Alatas brothers?" Sam asked, not sure if he wanted to know the answer. "They're high-vis officers in one of the most influential and powerful parts of the North Korean military, which means they live with advantages and benefits that most people in the country could never dream of seeing. Why would they bother going so far to meet a bunch of terrorists?"

Lucero pinned him with a look. "Because Colonel Kam has become a victim of his own success. His accomplishments and leadership skills have earned him the loyalty and admiration of a large segment of the military and its supporting industrial and scientific communities. Unfortunately for him, being that respected in North Korea tends to get you the wrong kind of attention from the powers that be in the Workers' Party. They've already started to view him as a threat, and it's widely believed that it's only a matter of time until someone comes up with a reason to drag him in front of a firing squad for crimes against the regime. Shortly after that, Major Tae and the totality of Kam's inner circle of soldiers and scientists will simply disappear."

"Crap," Lane breathed. "He's looking at an execution because he's good at his job? That sucks."

Lucero nodded. "It appears that Colonel Kam would agree with you. That's why he was on that island in the middle of nowhere meeting with terrorists."

"Meaning?" prompted Holden as Lucero paused to flip through more slides.

Lucero stopped on a blurry image filled with fine black lines and strange looking symbols before looking at them. "Meaning that the Colonel has a retirement plan for himself and his men. And the Alatas brothers are going to be funding that plan."

Dalton and Chasen both got up and moved closer to the monitor, leaning forward like they thought that would help them identify the image on the screen. Sam could have told them it wouldn't.

"What are we looking at?" Dalton asked.

"According to our subject matter experts, you're looking at a neutron generator," Lucero said. "It's a linear particle accelerator used to help start a nuclear fusion reaction. I understand it has multiple industrial applications, but in this case, it's used to trigger the reaction in a nuclear bomb."

"Shit," Sam muttered. "Kam and his soldiers were on that island to negotiate the price for a nuclear bomb? He's selling the Alatas brothers a North Korean nuclear weapon?"

Lucero nodded, a grim look on his face.

"Unfortunately, yes. And it's our job to stop it from happening."

"Holden told me that you've started seeing someone," Chasen remarked as he fell into step beside Sam outside the conference room.

After Lucero had dropped the figurative bomb on them, they'd spent another hour going over details on Colonel Kam and the Alatas brothers trying to find something that might help them figure out what the bad guys' next move might be, but it had largely been a waste of time. They simply didn't have enough intel to build a reasonable plan. And they wouldn't, not until someone came up with info on where and when this nuclear weapon buy was going down.

"Yeah," Sam said. "I only met her few days ago, but we've really hit it off. I'm seeing her again tonight actually."

"She sounds great," Chasen said with a smile, and for some reason, Sam appreciated that acknowledgment. "You bringing her to the cookout at your parents' place next Saturday? That way, we can all meet her."

Sam grimaced. His dad had been part of SEAL Team 5 for a long time and had only recently retired, but he was still involved with the team as a support contractor and instructor. Sam's parents still held regular cookouts every month like he did when his father was active duty.

"I'm not sure," Sam admitted. "She has no idea I'm a SEAL and I'm not sure I'm ready to throw her in the deep end of the pool before I know what we could have together."

Chasen was silent for a moment, like he was considering that. "I get it. But your Team is part of who you are. If you want her to be in your life, she needs to be aware of that side of things. Besides, your mom will make sure that everyone behaves and treats your girlfriend right."

Sam had no doubt about that. "I'll think about it."

As they left the secured part of the building, Sam stopped by the storage locker to pick up his phone—cells weren't allowed in the classified area. He pulled up Google to look for a cool place to take

Poppy out to dinner when his phone dinged with a text notification.

It was Poppy.

Want to come over to my apartment for dinner tonight? I'm make something simple and we can just relax and hang out here.

Just like that, the pressure to come up with some way to top last night's romantic picnic disappeared, replaced by warm thoughts of simply spending time with the woman he was quickly falling for.

Sam grinned.

Sounds like a plan, he texted back. *What time do you want me there and do I need to bring anything?*

CHAPTER
Five

POPPY WAS SO LOST IN THE THOUGHTS SWIRLING through her head that she almost missed the knock at the door. A glance at the clock on the stove told her it was exactly five o'clock, which was when they'd agreed Sam would show up for dinner. Something told her that he was the kind of man who liked to be on time.

"Hold on," she called. "Be right there."

She gave the creamy chicken alfredo another stir before turning down the heat to let it simmer and topping it with a glass lid. After checking to make sure the garlic bread wasn't burning, she then quickly made her way across the living room, running her hands down her dress as she went.

Poppy was rarely concerned about stuff like making an impression on a guy. With the majority of men dismissing her because she was a nerd, she'd gotten used to not caring what any of them thought of her. Or at least she's told herself that. But she could admit that with Sam, it was different. They'd only known each other a few days, but she already liked him. A lot. And she wanted him to like her as much.

She paused at the door to take a peek out the peephole, just to be safe. The sight of Sam standing there in a button-down and jeans took her breath away. The man was yummy beyond description.

How the hell had she gotten so lucky to have someone like him move in across the hall from her? She was pretty sure another guy had lived there before Sam, but for the life of her, Poppy couldn't remember what he looked like.

"Hey, there," Poppy said, a smile tugging the corners of her lips up as she opened the door and stepped back to let him in. "Right on time."

Sam stood there for a second, blatantly taking her all in. And yeah, she definitely liked the hungry expression that crossed his face when his eyes caught a look at the length of leg exposed by her boho dress. Still, even with all the heat, she couldn't help but notice that his eyes quickly snapped up and locked with hers after a few seconds. Seriously, did they make them like this anymore?

It was only after Sam stepped inside that she noticed the wine and flowers in his hands. She almost said something about him not needing to bring anything for the dinner, but then her eyes locked on the bouquet and all rational thoughts deserted her. No one had ever brought her flowers before. She never actually expected them, assuming it was an old-fashioned thing that nobody did anymore. But when she recognized the bright red poppies floating in with a nest of baby's breath, she damn near swooned.

He'd brought her poppies?

Holy cupcakes with sprinkles!

"They're beautiful," she whispered, reaching out to take them from him. "Let me put these in water."

Crap, what was she going to put them in? She didn't even own a vase.

Poppy ended up using a glass pitcher that Nyla had brought over once for a margarita party and ended up leaving behind when the both of them had gotten too blitzed to think straight.

"I'm not a connoisseur of wine, but the woman

at the store promised this chardonnay was a good choice," he said as she put the flowers on the table.

"I'll have to take her opinion then," Poppy said with a laugh. "I know almost nothing about wine beyond white goes with chicken and red goes with beef. Though it's possible I might have that backwards."

He flashed her a grin. "Well, whatever we're having, it smells delicious."

Poppy got him working on opening the wine while she checked the food. The lightly seasoned garlic bread was done and immediately went into a wicker basket with a microwave-warmed dish-towel in it—a trick her mom taught her to keep it fresh. Then she took the lid off the alfredo to let it thicken up before turning her attention to the angel hair pasta, which had cooked as quickly as she'd expected.

"There's salad in the fridge if you want to put it on the table," she said, carrying the pasta over to the sink to drain it. "I have a couple different kinds of dressings in there, too, since I wasn't sure what you liked."

For the next few minutes, they moved around each other in the kitchen without a single misstep.

Like they'd done it before a hundred times. When they finally sat down at the small table in the open area between the kitchen and living room, Sam raised his wine glass in a toast.

"Thank you for making dinner," he said with a smile. "I was trying to come up with an idea of where we should go tonight when you texted me with the invite. It was the perfect suggestion."

She gently touched her glass to his. "I'm glad you were cool with it. I would have been okay with going out somewhere again, but thought a low-key evening at home would be fun, too."

He took a bite of chicken and pasta, letting out an audible moan of appreciation, making Poppy smile. While she loved to cook, part of the reason she'd wanted to make dinner was to see him enjoy it.

"How was work this morning?" she asked as she speared a tomato with her fork.

"Not bad," Sam said after finishing the bite he'd just taken. "We just had to sit through a short briefing. I spent most of the morning hanging out with my Teammates getting ribbed about having a new girlfriend they didn't know anything about."

Something warm bubbled up in her chest

then, and it took Poppy a few moments to figure out what it was. At first, she assumed it was simply the fact that he'd told his Teammates about her. Then it struck her that he'd referred to her as his *girlfriend*. The word bounced around in her head for a while, generating emotions she couldn't remember ever feeling. But that was probably because she'd never been anyone's girlfriend before. Someone's date, yes. A friend with benefits, yes. But not a *real* girlfriend.

"So, you told them about me, huh?" Poppy grinned. "Only good things I hope."

"As if there's anything bad I could come up with," he said with a chuckle. "I told them that I'd met someone beautiful and intelligent. Their only comment was that if you were so intelligent why would you be going out with me."

As they ate, Sam went into more detail about his friends and Poppy couldn't help laughing more than a few times as he repeated what he'd told them about her, and their playful teasing in return. She and Nyla were close, but other than that, she'd never had any friendship like the kind Sam described with his buddies.

"It sounds like you and your Teammates are really close," she said, sipping her wine.

He smiled, helping himself to chicken and pasta. "That obvious, huh? But yeah, they're more like brothers than Teammates really. The bonds you develop with the people you work with are one of the things I love most about being in the Navy. I saw that with my dad and his Teammates, so it was a big part of why I joined."

She twirled some pasta around her fork. "Your dad was in the Navy, too? Was he a machinist mate like you?"

Sam hesitated for a moment, and she wondered if she'd touched on a sore subject, but then he grinned. "Yeah, he did the same thing as me. Retired less than a year ago from Coronado actually."

"It must have been cool growing up with a dad in the Navy," she said.

He poured a little more wine into her glass and then his own. "I guess that in the beginning—when I was a little kid—it was like that. I mean, my dad wore a uniform, like some superhero in the movies or a comic book. But as I got older, what really stuck with me was the sense of camaraderie

I saw between my dad and his Teammates. He'd do anything for them and vice versa. I knew deep down that the guys my father worked with would be there for my family and me as much as they were for him, and always will be. That realization stuck with me."

Poppy compared that to how she'd grown up. As a mechanic, her dad had worn a uniform of sorts, and to the people who needed their cars fixed, he was definitely a superhero. But while he'd occasionally had coworkers over for dinner or to watch a game on their big TV, it had never felt like any kind of extended family. They were merely coworkers.

"That sounds amazing," she said. "But having him deploy had to suck, I guess."

"Yeah, it did." Sam frowned down at his plate. "Dad was away frequently when I was a kid. Floats could last anywhere from six to nine months at a time, and those happened every couple years. But there were also special mission deployments. Those weren't as long, but they happened all the time. In between those, there were training exercises, many of them no-notice. I got used to seeing my dad at breakfast and then coming home from school to have my mom tell me he had to go somewhere."

It was her turn to frown. "That must have been hard."

She realized how much she'd overlooked what it was like to have her dad at home when she was little. It was something she'd taken for granted.

Sam pushed his empty plate and salad bowl back a little from the edge of the table. "I won't lie. Sometimes, it seriously sucked. When you're a kid, especially a young teenager, there are times you just need your dad there to talk to, you know? Then there were birthdays, Christmas, and the football game when you played in the state finals. But he couldn't be there for a lot of those."

Poppy came to another realization then that sometimes, people didn't realize just how difficult it was for the military families. She definitely wouldn't have been as strong as Sam obviously was as a kid.

The corner of Sam's mouth edged up. "But we dealt with it as a family. My mom is the rock of the family. She kept it together for me, my brothers, and sister. Truthfully, she's the real superhero, which is something my dad would agree with."

Poppy blinked. "You have siblings? I didn't know that! Why didn't you say anything before now?"

He chuckled. "It's not like I was trying to hide it, even if they are huge pains in my ass most of the time. Madison is the baby of the family. She's fifteen going on thirty, and scarily similar to my mother. Kayden and Ashton are twins. They're almost seventeen going on five. I love them to death, but wouldn't leave them alone in an empty tool shed for more than ten minutes because they'd find a way to blow it up."

Poppy laughed. She'd always wanted a brother or sister, but she was an only child. "They sound like a handful. I hope I can meet them sometime."

"Oh, you will," Sam promised. "As a matter of fact, my parents are holding a cookout at their house next Saturday. A bunch of people from my Team will be there, along with my sister and brothers. If you're cool with it, I'd love for you to come, too. We don't have to stay long, but I'd really like to introduce you to my parents."

Poppy sat, fork dangling loosely in one hand, praying her mouth wasn't hanging open like a carp. He wanted her to meet his parents. She couldn't think of anything she'd rather do!

"I'd love to go to the cookout with you," she said softly, fighting the urge to giggle. Instead, she focused on gathering up the empty plates littering the table, looking over at Sam carefully so he wouldn't realize how incredibly excited she was about something he likely thought of as trivial.

Then again, when Poppy saw the size of the smile that crossed Sam's face at her answer as he helped her clean the table, she started thinking maybe he was as thrilled at the possibilities as she was.

CHAPTER
Six

"YOU MADE TIRAMISU?" SAM ASKED, HIS EYES OPEN wide like it was Christmas morning and he'd just walked downstairs to see all the presents under the tree. And it was adorable.

Poppy laughed as she set down two plates on the coffee table, the square of cocoa powder covered cake on Sam's dish twice the side of hers. "I should probably fib and say I made it, but I picked it up at the bakery. Every time I try to make tiramisu, it comes out more like a thick pudding than a cake."

Beside her on the couch, Sam took a bite, rolling his eyes in pleasure. "You're talking to a guy who eats every meal out of a takeout bag or from a microwavable container. You could have fed me beef jerky and Twinkies and still come out ahead."

Poppy laughed again, wondering for about the fiftieth time how she'd been so lucky to stumble over Sam. Being with him was so easy and fun.

"I wish you would have mentioned that before," she said with a fake groan of disappointment. "I walked right past the rack of Slim Jim at the store. Think of all the time I could have saved making dinner."

He took another big bite of cake. "Slim Jim alfredo with pasta? That could work. You might want to lay claim to the credit now before someone else figures it out."

Poppy snorted so hard she almost choked on the creamy, cheesy goodness of the tiramisu filling. She didn't complain as Sam soothingly rubbed her back with his big hand. Yeah, it was nice.

As they ate dessert, the conversation turned into a random listing of their favorite supermarket junk food, which then somehow became a friendly debate where they attempted to convince each other that one particular favorite was better than the other.

"Little Debbie Cosmic Brownies are fudgy chocolate, covered with chocolate icing, sprinkled with dayglow colored chocolate chips," she stated firmly. "There is actually no way you can get more chocolate per square inch anywhere in the universe—not legally anyway. I win. Period. The end."

Sam let out a snort. "Please!"

He'd long since finished his piece of cake and some of hers, too, then slid both plates to the far end of the coffee table, like he felt they might need the space soon. She could only hope.

"Hostess Powdered Mini Donuts are junk food royalty," he added in a serious voice, like he was arguing his case in front of the Supreme Court. "They're soft, yummy, and covered with enough sugar to jumpstart a herd of narcoleptic elephants. It's also been scientifically proven that you can't eat just one, so there is absolutely no guilt when you eat the entire bag for breakfast."

Poppy laughed so much it hurt, and before she knew it, she was climbing onto Sam's lap, not sure if it was his idea or hers. She pulled the hem of her boho-print dress up to mid-thigh so it was easier to straddle his legs.

"You're amazing," she said softly, her body warming from the heat in his gaze. "You know that?"

"I think that's my line," he whispered, one

toy. At least not until she felt that familiar tingle building up between her legs. If she didn't stop, she'd orgasm right here on his lap.

Poppy pulled back slightly, trying to break contact between her throbbing clit and his jean-covered cock. But Sam grasped her hips, trapping her right where she was as he leaned back on the couch.

"Don't stop," he said, his gaze locking with hers, the heat there bringing a rush of warmth to her face. But even if it was a bit out of character to do anything this forward, she couldn't imagine stopping now, not with the way he was urging her on.

She spread her knees a little wider, pressing against his hard-on. What she wouldn't give to have him naked right then.

Unfortunately, Sam wasn't naked, so she'd just have to make do. Not that it was a problem, since the tingles between her thighs were already building up to dangerous levels.

Gyrating on Sam's lap while she held onto his shoulders to keep her steady, getting herself off while he watched was positively sublime. It was light years beyond anything she'd ever dreamed of doing, but the thought of stopping never entered her mind.

The orgasm hit Poppy hard, going from tingles to body-shaking spasms in the space of a few heartbeats. It was Sam's firm hands on her hips that kept her going, pulling her against him as her vision whited out and her throat ran raw from keening out her pleasure.

When she came back to the realm of rational thought, Poppy was a little surprised to find that she'd collapsed onto Sam's broad chest, his arms around her and her face buried in the curve of his neck. Yummy shoulder muscles had somehow found themselves between her lightly clenched teeth. Sam didn't complain. Instead, he sat there letting her regain control. When she finally pulled back to look down at him, there was something indescribable in his eyes. Something that did crazy things to her insides. Even more crazy than her recent orgasm.

"Do you know how beautiful you are right now?" he asked huskily. "Or how spectacular you looked as you came on my lap?"

There was a thud that was probably audible only to Poppy. And yeah, she was pretty sure it was her heart. It wasn't supposed to happen this fast. It probably shouldn't. Yet, there it was.

Poppy slithered off his lap, partly because she thought it would be sexy, and partly because she was still limp and boneless after riding the bus to orgasm town. On the way down, she grabbed his belt, popping the buckle and the buttons underneath with no problem. Getting his jeans and underwear down over his hard-on took a bit more effort, but she was determined, and Sam lifted his hips to make it easier. He laughed when she tossed them across the living room.

It wasn't like Poppy had mountains of experience when it came to the male form, but something told her that he was worthy of worship. All lean muscle, his shaft was long, thick, and slightly curved. She was pretty sure Sam was going to ruin her for all other men.

Dropping to her knees on the floor between his legs, she leaned forward to swipe her tongue across that perfect tip. The taste of him made her groan, and she wrapped her hand around him, squeezing gently. She scratched the nails of her free hand down his bare thigh, reveling in the feel of him tensing under her touch.

"Yes," Sam groaned.

The sound drove a spike of pure pleasure through Poppy's midsection, making it difficult to think about anything but getting him to come as hard as she had. Taking that as a challenge, she brought both hands up to wrap around the lower part of his erection, her mouth moving down to meet them, her tongue flicking at the sensitive underside of the head at the same time. The intoxicating feeling it gave her was hard to explain, but if she had her way, she'd do this for the rest of the night.

Sam's hand found its way into her hair, not trying to control her movements, but simply so he could tease his fingers along her scalp and neck, encouraging her to keep going. He seemed ready to come any second.

But just when she felt him stiffen under her tongue, the hand in her hair tightened, and Sam gently tugged her up and off his cock. She started to complain, but he dragged her upright, silencing her with a kiss.

"Not that I wasn't enjoying what you were doing," he murmured against her lips. "But the first time I come with you, I want to be buried deep inside."

Poppy considered making a crack about him having been buried pretty deep inside her mouth, but when he scooped her off her feet, she decided it could wait. Truthfully, she was looking forward to having him between her thighs, too.

The walk to her bedroom took seconds and then she was flying through the air, bouncing at least a foot off the mattress of her big comfy bed when she landed, laughing harder than she could ever remember laughing.

"Condom?" Sam asked, his voice a little desperate, like he thought he might have to run across the hallway naked to get a box from his place. She was tempted to let him just so she could see that muscular butt bounce when he ran.

"Nightstand. Top drawer," she said, pointing. "I picked up a few when I went food shopping. I wanted to be prepared."

He opened the drawer and pulled out an economy sized box, then lifted a brow in her direction. "I'm not sure if I should be thrilled that you think we need so many or terrified at the unrealistic expectations you apparently have when it comes to the stamina of a human male."

Poppy slid off her barely-there panties with a little butt wiggle. "Don't worry. I promise to keep my expectations firmly under control. I like to buy in bulk for the savings. Math—remember?"

Sam chuckled and tossed the box in the drawer, one of those cost-efficient condoms in hand. Quickly unbuttoning his shirt with his free hand, he shrugged it off, revealing the rest of his perfect body. Abs for days, a lithe, lean swimmer's body, smooth chest, and a furry little happy trail that had her ready to sink back down to her knees so she could run her face along it.

It should be illegal for any man to look this good.

Poppy watched as Sam rolled the condom down his thick shaft, which hadn't flagged in the least throughout their banter. If anything, he was even harder than he'd been during the blow job she'd been giving him.

Too eager to wait, Poppy crawled to the side of the bed, wiggling around until her butt was perched on the edge, toes barely touching the floor. When she spread her legs wide, Sam eagerly stepped between them. The bed was higher than most, putting her body at the perfect height.

Poppy shifted her hips a little, leaning back some as he slipped his hands under her knees, spreading her even further. With his hands busy, she wrapped her fingers around him, teasing the head up and down her folds. Her moan of anticipation turned into full-throated gasp as he slid in deep. She could feel him all the way down to her soul.

"Oh, yes," she breathed. "That feels so good."

She was practically hyperventilating by the time Sam bottomed out inside her, touching places that had never been touched before. Then he stayed there until she could feel him throbbing inside her. She expected him to start thrusting—because she was more than ready—but instead, Sam carefully wrapped her legs around his hips, making sure she had her ankles locked there before leaning forward to kiss her.

The tenderness of the kiss was the perfect complement to the intensity of him being inside her—soft and hard at the same time. She soon got lost in the sensation of his tongue tracing her lips, his teeth nipping at her lower lip, and wondering where that amazing mouth would go next. Then Sam started to move and thinking became impossible.

He thrust slowly to start, pulling back just a little before plunging back in. Each pump of his hips did something crazy to her, sending deep seismic shocks through her core, building and building until Poppy thought she might shake apart.

Then he found her clit with his thumb, pressing down firmly at the same time. There were no words to describe it. Having the most sensitive part of her body massaged at the same time he pumped deep inside her was beyond amazing.

It was impossible to tell where her orgasm started, deep inside where his shaft was hitting her G-spot, or at her clit, which his thumb was deliciously teasing. Either way, the spasm of pleasure burst out of her so wildly that she screamed without sound, her entire body locking up at once as her mind overloaded and went into reset mode.

Sam held her through her whole climax, one big hand around the back of her neck, the other splayed wide on her stomach, that thumb of his doing horribly wonderful, nearly evil, totally delightful things to her clit.

She was beating a rhythmic tattoo on his lower back with her heels when he suddenly picked her up. The next thing she knew, her back was against the wall near the door and Sam was pounding into her like he was possessed.

And it was spectacular.

Poppy wrapped tighter around him and held on like a Koala in a typhoon, burying her face in his shoulder and enjoying the moment. It was like something from a dream. A very sexy, X-rated dream. Or maybe something from one of the steamier romance novels she loved to read even as she told herself they were complete BS.

But this was real.

Oh, man, was it real.

She didn't quite have another orgasm. But when Sam slammed deep into her and groaned out his own climax, she definitely experienced a moment nearly as good as one. Everything inside her locked around him, and she swore she could feel his heat pouring into her even though he was wearing a condom.

A minute passed.

Or maybe it was an hour.

But at some point, Sam pulled back to look at

her, his smoldering gaze locking on hers. It was too soon for the words, but if she was of a mind to say them, she would have been serious, and they would have been oh-so-very real.

"Have I told you how amazing you are?" he whispered, his breath warm against her face as he continued to hold her firmly against the wall.

She smiled and kissed him. "Yes. Just a few minutes ago, as a matter of fact. But feel free to say it as often as you like."

CHAPTER
Seven

POPPY WAS SO NERVOUS SHE WAS PRACTICALLY BOUNCING on the seat of Sam's truck, toes tapping the floor in time with the song on the radio, her right hand repeatedly gripping and releasing the door handle. Out of the corner of her eye, she saw Sam glance her way occasionally, like he was worried she was going to shove open the door and jump out.

"You know, there's no reason for you to be worried," he said with a smile in her direction. "My mom and dad—as well as everyone else—are going to absolutely love you."

"I wish I could be as sure of that as you are."

Poppy wished she wasn't so worried about the party. It wasn't like her. She hadn't worried about what people thought of her in years. Not since she was a little kid and realized she'd never be like everyone else.

But everything was different with Sam. This past week with him had been amazing. They'd spent every night together going out to eat, jogging, walking along the beach, or hanging out on the couch binging shows on Netflix. It didn't matter what they did, as long as they did it together. Sam ended up spending so much time at her place that he hadn't even opened most of the boxes sitting in the middle of his living room. He simply walked over in the morning to grab a fresh uniform and head straight to base from there.

The wild thing was that in all the time they'd spent together, they'd yet to run out of things to talk about. It was crazy how comfortable she was with him. And while she wasn't ready to use the L word in regard to what they had because it was way too early for that, she'd admit that sometimes, in the middle of the night, while she was gazing up at the ceiling in the darkness while he slept beside her, she could truly see herself making a life with him.

"Just relax and be yourself," Sam said for the third time since they'd gotten in his truck.

He probably thought he was being helpful, so how could she tell him that being herself might be the worst advice he could ever give? Especially since considering she had a long track record of people not being very impressed with Poppy McCoy.

He reached out to take her hand. "Poppy, it doesn't matter what anyone thinks, not even my parents. I know what I have with you. Nothing else is important."

She smiled at him, relaxing a little. "That makes me feel better, but I still want to make a good impression on your family and your Teammates. I know how close you are with them."

Sam's smile faded as he turned his attention back to the road. Crap, had she said the wrong thing?

She squeezed his hand, but didn't say anything, instead thinking about what she'd say when she met his mother and father. As worried as she was about everyone else, Sam's parents had her petrified. Somehow, she needed to simply bowl them over.

Poppy was so focused on coming up with a list of things she should remember to say to them that she didn't realize they'd arrived at his parents' home until he pulled into the driveway. Sam was around and helping her out the truck before she had a chance to start hyperventilating too badly. Giving her a smile, he placed a warm hand on her lower back as they walked toward the porch, a tray of fudge brownies they'd made for the cookout in her hand.

She only had a few seconds to take in the two-story brick and stucco home before she and Sam were at the front door, but Poppy couldn't help thinking she'd seen this place before.

"Poppy...um...there's something we need to talk about before we go inside," Sam said, his voice coming out hesitantly and lacking the confidence normally there. "I know I should have told you earlier, but I couldn't seem to find the right time and place. Or words, to be honest."

Tension made her stomach clench again. And this time, it had nothing to do with meeting his parents. "What's wrong?"

"Nothing," he murmured. "It's just that..."

Before he could say more, the door opened, interrupting him and startling Poppy so much that she nearly dumped brownies all over the place.

"What the hell are you two doing standing out here on the porch talking when there's a whole backyard full of people waiting to see you?"

Poppy spun around to see a tall, well-built man standing there holding the door open, smiling at them. "You must be the mysterious girl-friend Sam has been telling everyone about that half of us thought he made up. I'm happy to see he's not delusional. It'd be hard to hold onto a security clearance if he was. I'm Lane, by the way." His gaze dropped to the tray in her hands. "Are those brownies? I love brownies." When she and Sam still just stood there, he frowned. "Dude, you guys coming inside or what?"

Sam pinned his friend with a look. "Give us a minute, huh? I need to talk to Poppy first. We'll be right in."

Lane snorted. "Forget it, Dude. Did you miss the part where I said that everyone's waiting to meet your girlfriend? If I don't show up with you guys in the next sixty seconds, the whole Team is going to be out here, along with your mom and dad. So, stow the romantic chatter until later and let's go."

Before Sam could say anything, Lane stepped

out of the doorway and herded them inside like a couple of cats. Poppy started to laugh, but the sound quickly got stuck in her throat as she abruptly remembered why she'd recognized the home. She'd been here before. At one of the lowest moments of her life.

Crap.

Sam took her hand, slowing her down a little as they followed Lane toward the sliding glass doors that led to the backyard. "I need to tell you something before we go outside. I swear I never meant to hide this from you, but I didn't want to mess up what we had."

Lane was already through the door, announcing their arrival to what sounded like fifty people. Poppy had no idea what Sam was going on about, but as she hesitated in the middle of the all-too-familiar living room, she knew she had to tell him about the last time she'd been at his parents' house before everything blew up in her face.

"I'm a Navy SEAL," he blurted out before she could even think about how to start her own confession.

One moment, Poppy was staring at him in shock, and the next, Lane reached back into the house and grabbed her hand, dragging her and Sam out onto the big deck overlooking a perfectly manicured back yard with half a dozen picnic tables and a seemingly endless amount of lawn chairs.

"Everybody, this is Poppy," Lane called in a loud voice. "She's actually real, so to all relevant parties, pay up!"

Poppy ignored Lane—and Sam for that matter. Instead, she gazed out across the yard, surprised at how many of the people she still recognized, even though almost a year had passed since she'd sat at one of those very same tables making a total idiot of herself.

The first person that caught her attention was Dalton. Because, of course.

He stared at her, his face going pale as she stood there rigid as a board, watching first confusion and then something that might have been terror cross his face. Poppy wondered if it was the realization that he'd slept with the woman that Sam was dating or if there was something else freaking him out.

She got her answer when an attractive blond woman walked over to Dalton and handed him a beer before casually wrapping an arm around his waist. A moment later, a little girl with dark blond hair tied up in a ponytail raced across the yard to join him and the woman. The smiles on the trio's faces—along with the wedding rings on the couple's left hands—filled in the blanks.

Dalton was married to a woman with a kid.

That certainly explained why he looked so uptight to see her. He was probably worried she'd make a scene and blow what he had with his new family.

If only she could tell him that was the furthest thing from her mind.

"Poppy, this is Wes and his girlfriend, Kyla," Sam said, interrupting her thoughts and forcing her attention to the dark haired, blue-eyed guy and the petite, pretty girl standing in front of them. "He's one of my best friends on the Team."

Poppy went on automatic pilot, shaking hands and greeting people, even taking the hard seltzer someone offered her. There were Hayley and Chasen Ward, who'd gotten married since she'd seen them last, followed by a whole string of SEALs who'd been at the previous cookout Dalton had brought her to. Thankfully, all of them acted like they were meeting her for the very first time or things would have been even more awkward than they already were. And in a way, she supposed they *were* meeting the real her for the first time.

It was kind of like she was meeting each of them for the first time, too. Besides Hayley and Chasen, she hadn't remembered any of their names. Then again, at the time, she'd been more focused on playing the vapid airhead Dalton had thought she was. She cringed as she remembered making some seriously insipid comments to Hayley about how Chasen had rescued her from terrorists in Africa like a character in a romance book. One look at Hayley's face told her that the woman still remembered every single regrettable word.

"And this is my mom, Melissa, and my dad, Kurt," Sam said as they came to a stop in of his parents, neither of whom looked thrilled to see her. "Mom, Dad. This is Poppy McCoy, my girlfriend."

Poppy held her breath as she shook each of their hands, waiting for the sky to fall. Any second now, Sam's mother would start ranting about her son bringing home a bimbo stripper. Because, as far as Melissa knew, that's exactly who Poppy was when she'd been with Dalton.

Kurt, who looked like an older version of Sam, said it was nice to meet her.

"We've heard a lot about you," Melissa said with far more calm than Poppy expected. An elementary school teacher, she had dark eyes and wore her brunette hair up in a messy bun. "You're a math professor at San Diego Mesa College, right?"

Poppy froze, unable to speak. Was this Melissa's way of saying she was going to cover for her? Or was the woman expecting her to "come clean" about the whole stripper thing when she'd very briefly dated Dalton?

"Yes," Poppy said, finally finding her voice. "I've been teaching there for almost a year and a half now."

Maybe it was the tone of Poppy's voice or the fact that she wasn't using the airhead vocals she'd put on when she was with Dalton, but either way, Melissa's gaze sharpened considerably.

Poppy glanced at Sam out the corner of her eye. From the look on his face, he was picking up on the strange vibe going on between her and his parents. She opened her mouth, ready to put it all out there, but before she could say anything, half a dozen cell phones rang, including Sam's, making most of the women jump in alarm.

Cursing under his breath, Sam pulled his phone from his pocket. "Travers."

After that, there wasn't much in the way of conversation on Sam's part. A few grunts here and there, then, "Roger that."

The expression that crossed Sam's face as he shoved the phone back in his jeans was a cross between worry and fear. And it scared the hell out of Poppy.

"I have to go," he said, leaning in to kiss the corner of her mouth, then handing her the key to his truck. All around the backyard, the other SEALs who'd just gotten phone calls were busy saying their goodbyes to their significant others. "I'll catch a ride with Lane and will call you as soon as I can."

Head suddenly spinning, Poppy clutched the key in her hand as she watched Dalton give his wife and little girl a kiss and a hug. A few feet away, Kyla was kissing Wes almost desperately, while Hayley murmured, "safe and sound," to Chasen as she hugged him tightly.

Poppy turned back to Sam, grabbing his hand and holding him in place even as Lane stood off to the side waiting impatiently for him. "What do you mean, you have to go? Who was that call from? Where are you going? When are you coming back?"

He grimaced. "Crap, this is all stuff I should have told you before. About me being a SEAL, I mean. That was a call from headquarters telling us that we have a mission. I can't tell you where I'm going because I don't know. And even if I did, I couldn't tell you. It's classified."

Poppy nearly mentioned that she almost certainly had a higher security clearance than he did, but bit her tongue. That obviously wasn't something she could get into right now—or ever for that matter. But the idea that the Navy could simply call Sam out of the blue and send him off to who knew where didn't sit well with her.

"I'm so sorry I didn't tell you about the SEAL thing earlier, but I was worried you'd bail on me without giving me chance," Sam said, both his tone and expression conveying all kinds of anguish that hurt her to see. "But right now, I have to go. I don't have a choice."

She wanted to ask him so many more

questions, but then Sam was kissing the air from her lungs and the sense from her head.

"I promise we'll talk when I get back," he said before disappearing into the house with Lane.

Poppy stood there, transfixed by the sliding glass doors Sam had disappeared through, trying to comprehend everything that had just happened. But as good as she might be with math and all things logical, this moment escaped her. Sam was a Navy SEAL. Now, he was off to who knew where, probably doing something that could get him killed.

It struck her then how much Sam had come to mean to her, and in such an incredibly short period of time, too. Something tugged at her heart, and she found herself wishing she'd said something to him about it. She told herself that she'd get the chance, that Sam would be fine. But then she started thinking about all the issues they'd have to deal with when he did come back. Yeah, the part where he'd lied about being a SEAL would be hard enough to handle, but how would he react when he figured out that she'd slept with one of his teammates? Or that his parents hated her?

Melissa gave Dalton's wife and daughter a

hug, then the woman took the little girl's hand and led her toward the sliding glass doors. Poppy supposed that meant they were leaving. The child, who'd been laughing and smiling a few minutes ago, now looked like all the life had been sucked out of her. Poor thing.

Letting out a sigh, Poppy turned to leave, too.

"Poppy, don't go."

She turned to see Kyla standing there with a concerned look on her face. Over by the grill, Kurt was serving burgers and hot dogs to the rest of the guests who were still there, even if the tone of the party was more subdued now.

"Stay, please," Kyla added softly. "Having the guys take off like that is scary. Being with other wives and girlfriends can make it a little easier."

"Kyla's right," Hayley said, stopping on her way to the picnic table up on the deck, a plate of food in her hand. "Stay so we can talk."

Beside Hayley, Melissa surprised Poppy by nodding.

Kyla gave her a smile. "Come on. Let's get something to eat."

Poppy wasn't very hungry, but she fell into step beside Kyla as the other woman headed for the grill. Melissa wouldn't invite her to stay if she wanted to chew her out, right? Maybe she'd come out of this whole thing okay.

"So," Melissa said after Poppy and Kyla joined her and Hayley with their plates, "I'm guessing you really are a college professor and not a stripper?"

Beside Poppy, Kyla gasped, her eyes wide as she looked back and forth between them. "Wait. What?"

Melissa didn't say anything, the questioning look she gave Poppy clearly saying she was genuinely interested in the answer. Even Hayley was regarding her curiously.

Needing a minute, Poppy sipped the iced tea she'd traded the hard seltzer for. She never drank alcohol if she had to drive, but right now, she wouldn't mind a little bit of liquid courage.

"No." She took a deep breath. "I got into a discussion with my best friend about men not being into smart women, and the next thing I know, I'm making a bet that I can snag the next attractive guy who walked into the club if I pretended to be an airhead stripper."

"And that guy was Dalton," Hayley said.

She nodded. "Yeah. Our relationship—if you could call it that—lasted a week."

Hayley sighed. "I wish I could say that surprises me, but I get the feeling that Dalton was like that. At least before Kimber and Emma."

"The woman and child you saw him with earlier," Melissa supplied. "It's a long story, but the short version is that Emma is his daughter and he married Kimber shortly after finding out."

Poppy didn't know what to think about that, other than maybe Dalton had grown up drastically since she'd known him.

"So, that whole performance you put on here at the cookout when you were here with Dalton was all an act?" Hayley asked.

Poppy nodded, nibbling on a Dorito. "That's the problem with pretending to be a ditz to land a guy. You're forced to stick with the act. I couldn't tell Dalton and after a few dates, everything fell apart and we went our separate ways."

Melissa considered that for a moment. "How did you meet my son?"

Poppy couldn't help smiling at the memory. "He moved into the apartment across the hall from mine and ended up dropping a box of his stuff while moving in. We ended up bonding over a Rubik's Cube."

Melissa laughed. "I didn't even know he still had that old thing."

"He has a lot of good memories about solving the puzzle with his dad," Poppy said.

"Sam told you about that, huh? He doesn't share stuff like that with people he's just met. I guess that means he's really fallen for you."

"The feeling is mutual," Poppy admitted, smiling again. "Though I have no idea why I'm telling you guys when I haven't even told Sam yet." Her smile faded and she gazed down at her plate. "I should have said something to him before he left."

Silence descended around the table. Poppy usually didn't mind being left alone with her thoughts, but after everything that had happened today, she couldn't stop her mind from heading in a dark direction.

"Sam and the other guys are going to be okay," Melissa suddenly said, interrupting Poppy's downward mental spiral. "They're well-trained and experienced. They're going to get through the mission and cover each other's backs, then come home to us safely. They're SEALs. That's what they do."

Poppy nodded, praying that was true. "It must be tough having to worry about your son being a SEAL after his dad retired from the Navy."

"It is." Melissa grimaced. "I really thought I was done with all this worry and stress when I finally convinced Kurt to retire, but now I have to do it all over again with Sam." She gave Poppy a small smile. "Except this time, it looks like I get to share my worries with you. And you get to share yours with me."

Logically, Poppy knew worry didn't work that way, but right then, sitting at this table with three other women who were going through the same thing she was, she decided that maybe she was wrong. Having someone to share the burden *did* help.

As they ate, they talked about being left behind while the guys went out on missions. It should have made Poppy more afraid for Sam, but instead, she found their support comforting at the same time.

"Has anyone thought about how awkward this mission is going to be if Dalton and Sam realize they've both slept with Poppy?" Hayley asked, a concerned expression on her face. "You know, guys being guys and all?"

Poppy cringed inwardly at the thought of Sam finding out about her and Dalton that way. The thought of how they'd behave toward each other during the mission hadn't entered her mind at all—until now. "You don't think they'd get into a fight, do you? They're friends."

Hayley and Kyla didn't say anything. Melissa, on the other hand, let out a snort of amusement. Or maybe derision. It was difficult to tell which.

"They might be friends, but they're also men who happen to possess a higher-than-normal amount of testosterone," Melissa said. "Which means it's almost a certainty they'll get into a fight. It's just a matter of whether it will be limited to words, or if fists will be involved."

Crap.

CHAPTER

MADURA ISLAND, LOCATED OFF THE NORTHEAST COAST of Java, was drastically larger than the postage stamp sized bit of sand that Kepulauan Nenusa had been, both in terms of real estate and population. Even so, Sam would never have guessed they were on an island of over three million people, not given the total silence enveloping this particular stretch of forest running along the northern edge of the place.

The return trip to Indonesia had been as rushed and exhausting as the first time. Sam had tried to sleep throughout most of the fifteen-hour flight to Jakarta on the unmarked military aircraft they'd taken, but the ride had been rough and the roar from the engines loud enough to require hearing protection. There had been a mission briefing on the plane followed by a short trip via helicopter out to a frigate cruising the Java Sea, where they'd gotten another briefing, and then a midnight boat ride to a deserted stretch of beach east of Sokabana.

In theory, the Alatas brothers ran some kind of training camp near here. The theory also held that the brothers were either here now or would show up sometime soon to finalize plans for the procurement of the nuclear weapon from Colonel Kam and the North Korean contingent. The idea was that Sam and the other SEALs would sneak into the camp and hear something that would tell them where the North Koreans would be and when they would be there.

Lucero and the CIA hadn't been very forthcoming about where they were getting their intel on the Alatas brothers, and based on the number of times the words *in theory*, *supposedly*, and *should be* had been used during the briefings, Sam wasn't too sure what he and his Teammates were going to run into out here in these woods. He only hoped this whole trip wasn't a waste. One that had possibly messed up his relationship with Poppy.

Movement ahead of him caught his attention

and Sam looked up to see Dalton holding up a hand with a closed fist—standard military signal for all stop. He immediately dropped to one knee, swinging his NVGs to the right to scan his assigned sector, but there wasn't anything there. Wes, Lane, Holden, Chasen, Nash, and Noah were all out there somewhere. They were simply too good to be seen.

A few moments later, he heard Chasen on the radio, saying they'd reached the edges of the brothers' compound.

"Everyone hold tight while Nash and I scout out the perimeter to see what we've got," Chasen added.

The seconds turned into minutes, and with nothing to do but stare into the darkness at nothing, Sam found himself thinking about Poppy. No surprise there. He tended to think about her nearly every free moment of the day and night. And as he'd been doing a lot since the cookout gone wrong, he couldn't help but replay every moment of what happened at his parents' house.

He'd expected for her to freak out when he told her he was a SEAL. Instead, she'd looked around the backyard like she'd seen a ghost. All he could think was that she'd been so devastated to learn he'd lied to her about being a SEAL that she'd completely shut down.

That would certainly explain why she'd barely had a reaction when cell phones had started ringing. Sure, she'd been upset and asked the expected questions of who, where, and when, but he could tell from the distracted look on her face that she'd spoken those words purely on instinct. He doubted if she would have comprehended his answers even if he'd been able to give her any. It hurt like hell to think he'd hurt her so badly that her logical mind had stopped processing, but he couldn't come up with any other explanation.

When he heard the murmur of soft conversation, he realized Lane and Wes must have gotten bored waiting for Chasen to give them an update because both of them had moved from their positions in the Team's scattered formation close enough to talk to Dalton.

Sam took another look around to make sure they were alone, then moved forward to join his Teammates. They were a good quarter mile from the edge of the Alatas compound, so there was no reason to think they'd have security patrols out this far. Not without a known threat.

He was still fifteen feet away when he heard Dalton murmur something to Lane and Wes. He didn't catch all of it, but he was pretty sure the last part was, *should I tell Sam about Poppy?*

"Tell me what?" he asked softly, making all three of his buddies stand up and snap around with weapons raised.

Sam had to stop himself from instinctively lifting his own.

"What the hell are you doing sneaking up on people?" Wes hissed, looking around like he thought someone might be eavesdropping on the conversation. "You could have gotten yourself shot."

"I wasn't sneaking around," Sam said, moving closer and looking at Dalton. "What could you possibly have to tell me about Poppy?"

Everyone in the platoon knew that Dalton used to be a player. Before he'd reunited with Kimber, Dalton had hooked up with half the world's female population. Okay, maybe that was an exaggeration, but he dated a lot of women.

Dalton stared at him through his NVGs, then looked away, shifting nervously from one foot to the other. "Um...nothing. I was just saying how nice it was to finally meet Poppy."

The way Lane and Wes made a show of being interested in something in the surrounding darkness would have been comical if Sam didn't know for a fact that Dalton was lying.

"Dalton, if you have something to say about Poppy, just say it," Sam ground out. "If not, keep your mouth shut."

His Teammate glanced at Lane and Wes, something passing between them that obviously had his buddies worried. After several more seconds of silence, Sam cursed under his breath. But before he could blow, Dalton finally spoke.

"Yesterday isn't the first time I've met Poppy," his friend said, still not looking at Sam. "We knew each other before you came to Coronado."

"Okay," Sam said. "So?"

"So..." Dalton sighed. "I hate to be the one to tell you this, but you deserve to know. Poppy isn't a math professor at some college. She's a stripper."

Sam started to laugh, figuring his Teammates were still ragging on him about having a girlfriend, but then he realized Dalton was serious. He actually believed the crap he'd just said.

"You don't know what the hell you're talking about," Sam growled. "Poppy has a doctorate from UC Berkley. I've seen the degree mounted on the wall of her apartment, and I've driven her to work at the college several times, as well as seen her talking to her students."

Dalton shook his head. "Dude, she's playing you."

"Oh, yeah? What makes you think that?"

"Dammit, Sam," Dalton muttered. "I didn't just *know* her before. I slept with her. I mean she didn't even make me work for it. The minute she heard I was a SEAL, she was all over me. Dude, Poppy is a groupie."

Sam didn't even realize he was moving until his right fist slammed into Dalton's jaw. Then he was somehow on top of his friend, fists coming down over and over.

Dalton might have been caught off guard at first, but then he quickly fought back, a knee coming up to smash into Sam's ribs, a glancing blow from his fist catching him on the chin.

Sam had no idea how long the fight lasted, but it got loud and covered a significant stretch of jungle. He knew that because Dalton tried to smash his head into a tree trunk while Sam did his best to strangle his buddy with a nearby vine.

Everything was still a white-hot blur of anger when Sam felt heavy hands on his shoulders jerking him upright. Holden and Nash got a grip on Dalton, dragging him away from the scuffle. Sam lunged for him again, but Chasen yanked him back and gave him a rough shake.

"Chill the hell out!" his chief warned. "I wish I didn't know what this was all about, but unfortunately, I do. And guess what? I don't give a shit. I don't care what Dalton said. I don't care how you took it. I don't care about your hurt feelings or how insulted either of you might be."

Sam glared at Dalton, supremely satisfied to see that his Teammate was bleeding from a split lip and a cut above his left eyebrow. From the pain he was feeling along his own jaw, as well as the warm trickle trailing down his neck, Sam was pretty sure he wasn't much better off.

"You know what I do care about?" Chasen added, looking more pissed than Sam had ever seen him. "I care that we're barely four hundred meters from the edge of a heavily guard terrorist training compound and you two are out here brawling like two idiots in a bar fight. We're supposed to be finding out when these assholes are planning to buy a nuclear weapon so we can stop them, and you morons seem more interested in ghosting the rest of your Team and letting us get our asses killed."

Sam possessed at least enough maturity to feel embarrassed about his behavior, even if he still felt like punching Dalton.

"I'm putting you two together for the rest of this op, so you both need to pull your shit together and wire it tight," Chasen continued, the threat clear in his voice. "If you don't and this thing goes sideways because of the two of you, I'll effing leave the both of you on this island and you can swim your juvenile asses all the way back to the States."

Giving him and Dalton a hard look, Chasen turned and disappeared into the darkness. Sam glanced at Dalton to see that his Teammate was still just as pissed as he was. No one said a word as they followed Chasen toward the training compound.

The mission itself was almost anti-climactic after the fight in the jungle. Sam and the rest of his Team slipped into the fenced-in compound, easily making it past the four roving guards. They set up surveillance equipment on the main building as well as two other possible meeting locations, then they hid, Sam and Dalton squeezing under the flooring of one of the supply huts. The two of them were wedged in so close together that Sam could feel Dalton's body heat. Even though they were face to face, they didn't say a word to each other. They simply couldn't take the risk. If Sam got pissed off again and they started fighting, they'd be found out for sure.

So, Sam simply lay there in the dirt under the hut, nursing the aches from the recent fight, watching as the occasional spider or snake passed by on the way to who knew where. And the whole time they waited, praying some curious dog didn't crawl under the hut with them, Sam couldn't help but think about what Dalton had told him. As much as he knew the stripper stuff was all bullshit, he couldn't get past the part about Dalton having slept with the woman he'd been falling for. Sam knew it shouldn't matter, that Poppy was an adult who'd obviously slept with other men before him, but the fact that it was Dalton bothered him more than he would have ever imagined.

The sun was well above the horizon when the Alatas brothers showed and immediately headed for the main building. Sam and Dalton had no access to the surveillance feed from that location, so they were forced to wait for what seemed like forever until Chasen announced they had what they needed. The time and place with the weapon exchange had been set, and they had it all.

Unfortunately, everyone was forced to stay in hiding all day, until the gathering darkness gave them enough cover to escape, which sucked.

Sam would have liked to say he used the time to come up with something intelligent to say to Poppy, but as they boarded another unmarked cargo plane back to the States a few hours later, he still had no idea what he was going to say when he saw her.

CHAPTER
Nine

S
AM MUST HAVE STOOD IN THE HALLWAY OUTSIDE
Poppy's apartment for at least ten minutes,
trying to figure out if he wanted to knock on
her door. But every time he worked up the courage
to do it, doubts would creep into his head, and he'd
change his mind.

"Maybe I should talk to her tomorrow," he
murmured out loud. "After I get some sleep."

That would probably be the best idea. The
flight back from Madura—with the time change
and dateline thrown in—had been murder.
Between his concerns about Poppy and the lecture
from hell he'd gotten from Chasen, he hadn't slept
a wink. He'd been running on fumes for nearly
forty hours with nothing more than a few cat naps
while he'd been stuck under that damn hut.

"Yeah, that's what I'm going to do," he said to the empty hallway. "I'm going to go to bed and talk to Poppy tomorrow. Maybe by then, I'll know what to say."

Satisfied with that plan, Sam turned for his apartment only to spin around when he heard Poppy's door open. Poppy stood there, looking tired but beautiful, wearing nothing but a ribbed tank top and a pair of skimpy sleep shorts. She probably just woke up, but damn, did she look good or what?

"Were you out here talking to yourself?" Poppy asked, looking up and down the hallway, like she was searching for confirmation to her question before he even answered.

It seemed like a simple question, and yet, Sam had no idea how to answer it. If he said yes, he'd come off like a whack job. If he said no, she'd want to know who he'd been talking to. Which would ultimately lead to the whack job conclusion.

Before he had a chance to reply one way or another, Poppy suddenly let out a gasp and took several quick steps toward him.

"What happened to your face?" she asked, her eyes wide with alarm as she tentatively reached out to gently cup his jaw. "You look like you got hit by a truck."

Sam prayed that Dalton never heard those words. His Teammate's blows had left bruises and abrasions all along his chin and the left side of his face, but Sam would never admit Dalton had gotten the best of him.

"It's nothing," he said, trying to sound casual. "These things happen sometimes during a mission. It's nothing I can talk about, and more importantly, it's not the reason I was standing in the hallway."

From the look Poppy gave him, Sam was sure she was about to argue the issue, but after a few seconds, she stepped back, holding the door of her apartment open for him. Sam released the breath he didn't realize he'd been holding. After the whole SEAL thing, he hadn't been sure she'd let him back into her life, much less her apartment.

Poppy closed the door behind him but didn't invite him further into her place. He guessed they'd talk here then.

"Why *were* you standing out in the hallway?" she asked, and Sam started a little, realizing he'd been standing there for several long heartbeats not saying a thing.

He blanked for a second, not sure what he wanted to say. Should he apologize about keeping the SEAL stuff from Poppy or ask her whether she'd slept with one of his Teammates? Apologies first. Accusations later.

"You and Dalton, huh?" he asked, cursing himself for asking even as the words came out of his mouth.

Sam started to retract the statement—if that was even possible—but he bit his tongue. It was too late for that.

Poppy stared at him, her expression unreadable. Finally, a defeated look crossed her face and she let out a long sigh, shoulders slumping. "You know about that?"

Whatever he expected her to say, it wasn't that. For some reason, the way she said the words—like she was more upset about being found out than anything else—sparked something inside him. He was exhausted mentally and physically, so it took him a few seconds to recognize the sensation roiling in his gut. But when it hit, he was shocked.

Jealousy.

Sam couldn't handle the fact that the woman he cared about had slept with one of his Teammates. He was jealous. It might be petty, juvenile, and ugly, but there it was all the same.

"Yeah, I know about that." He told himself to turn and walk out of her apartment before he said something he regretted, but instead, he kept talking. "Were you ever going to tell me that you'd slept with Dalton or did you want me to hear about it from him?"

Dammit.

It was like he was standing on the side of the road watching someone drive off a cliff. When had he become such a prick?

"And why exactly would I have ever brought up the time I dated some random SEAL?" Poppy demanded, her voice low and her eyes flashing dangerously. "When you went out of your way to convince me you were a machinist mate? It makes me wonder if we hadn't gone to your parents' house, would you still be lying to me about that?"

"This isn't about me telling you I'm a SEAL," he snapped. "This is about you sleeping with Dalton."

"Yeah, I slept with Dalton—a year before I ever met you." She sighed and ran her hand through her hair. "Look, I made a bet with a friend that if I acted like a bimbo stripper, any guy in the club we were in would pick me up in a hot minute. And Dalton picked me up."

Sam ground his jaw. "Dammit, I don't care why you pretended you were a stripper. I care that you slept with my Teammate."

She folded her arms and glared at him. "I've never asked who you slept with before you met me, and I can't go back and change who I slept with. If that's something you can't get past, then I don't think there's anything more to say."

"I guess there isn't," he said, the words coming out as if they were being spoken by someone Sam didn't even know.

Poppy walked into the kitchen and grabbed something from the counter. A moment later, she was back, holding out the keys to his truck. She dropped them in his hand, then moved over to the door, pulling it open and standing there without saying a word.

Sam stood there, a part of him demanding he say something—anything—that would fix this before it was too late. But after a few seconds, he realized there was nothing he could say that would make any of this better. He'd caught the bridge between him and Poppy on fire, then blew it up for good measure.

Cursing silently, he walked out.

The door slamming behind him put an exclamation point on what Sam knew was the end of everything he'd had with Poppy. He stood there for a long time in the hallway, replaying their horrible conversation over and over again in his head. Not ten minutes ago, he'd been working up the courage to knock on her door planning to apologize so they could straighten everything out. Now, he was stuck trying to figure out how things had gone so wrong. He still couldn't believe half the things he'd said to Poppy.

Walking over to his apartment, he unlocked the door, then stopped and looked back across the hall, wondering how he was supposed to live here now. To say running into Poppy in the stairwell was going to be awkward as hell was an understatement.

Inside his apartment, he took stock of all the boxes he'd yet to unpack, wondering if he should even bother when he might end up moving again.

Damn, what a mess.

CHAPTER
Ten

"YOU READY TO GIVE THE BRIEFING THIS MORNING?" Nyla asked, sounding all bright and cheerful as she walked into the break room, catching Poppy pouring a cup of coffee.

"Uh-huh," she murmured, slowly turning around to face her friend.

In truth, she had absolutely no desire to stand around for the next couple of hours talking to a bunch of CIA field agents about North Korean nuclear weapons. But that's what was on the agenda for this morning, so that's what she'd do.

"You look like you didn't sleep a wink last night," Nyla said with a frown that quickly turned into a knowing smile. "Never mind. Your hunky sailor came home last night, didn't he? No wonder you look so exhausted!"

Poppy sighed. She definitely hadn't gotten any sleep last night, but it wasn't because she was getting busy with anyone, that's for sure. "Yeah, Sam came home last night. But unfortunately, we ended up getting into a huge argument and broke up. I look like crap because I spent the whole night lying in bed staring at the ceiling trying to figure how everything fell apart so fast."

"What?!" Nyla's jaw dropped. "I thought everything was going great with you guys. I mean, besides the part about him not telling you that he's a SEAL. You told me the other day that you couldn't wait for him to get back so you could talk it all out."

"Yeah, that was the plan." She stared down at her coffee mug. It had always felt good to have a friend she could talk to about everything, but she never dreamed she'd have to tell Nyla something like this. "But it turns out all Sam wanted to talk about was the fact that I'd slept with one of his Teammates."

Nyla's eyes widened. "Dalton told him?"

Poppy nodded. "And Sam is fixated on the fact that I slept with the guy. He implied that I purposefully tried to hide it from him. Like it was some big conspiracy."

"Wait a second," Nyla said, a baffled look on her face. "He's pissed at you for a previous relationship you had with a SEAL when he's the one who lied to you about being one? Where the hell does he get off with that crap?"

"I don't know." Poppy sipped her coffee. "I never expected Sam to act like this. After we showed up at the cookout, I knew he'd find out about Dalton and me sooner or later, but I thought he'd handle it like an adult. When I realized he wasn't going to be able to get over it, I broke up with him."

Nyla took Poppy's mug out of her hand and set it on the counter, then pulled her in for a hug. "I'm sorry. I know you were hoping this time it would be different and that Sam wouldn't be like all the other jerks you've gone out with. I promise that it will work out with someone someday. You're going to find the right person."

Poppy returned her friend's hug and fought back tears. There'd been enough of those last night and again this morning before coming to work. She refused to cry over Sam anymore. He wasn't worth it. Or at least that's what she kept telling herself.

"But I thought Sam was the right person," she admitted softly. "Maybe it's time I accept that I don't know a damn thing about men. In which case, maybe I should just stop looking."

Nyla pulled back and gave her a stern look. "Don't you dare. Mr. Right is out there and you're going to find him."

Poppy was about to tease Nyla about her optimistic outlook on the world, when someone behind her cleared their throat. She turned to see Roy standing there.

"Sorry to interrupt, but your field operatives are here," he said. "I put them in briefing room two."

"Thanks, Roy," she said, then looked at Nyla as she picked up her coffee mug. "You're coming in for this right?"

"Wouldn't miss it for the world," Nyla said with a smile. "It's not every day that I get to be part of a mission to swipe a foreign nuclear weapon out from under a bunch of scary bad guys. And who knows, maybe one of those CIA agents will catch your eye and make you forget all about Sam and his crap."

Poppy shook her head but didn't say anything

as they headed down the hallway. Something told her it was going to take a long time to get over Sam.

Mug in hand, Poppy opened the door of the classified briefing room and led the way inside. CIA agent Keith Lucero was up front near the projection screen, waiting for her.

"Okay, everyone," Lucero said as Poppy walked to the front of the room. "I'd like to introduce the subject matter expert who will be briefing you on the objective for your next mission—Dr. Poppy McCoy."

Setting her mug on a table, Poppy turned to face her audience. When she saw the eight Navy SEALs seated at the conference table, all the air left her lungs.

Sam must have been as stunned to see her as she was to see him because he stared at her like he'd seen a ghost.

Out the corner of her eye, she saw an image appear on the large screen on the front wall. She didn't need to look at it to know it was the drawing of the North Korean nuke she'd put together by cutting and pasting half a dozen different photos taken during the earlier surveillance mission to Kepulauan Nenusa. Pictures she now knew Sam and his SEAL Teammates had taken.

Her head spun. The idea that Sam had been on that island risking himself to get this information did horrible things to her insides.

"Dr. McCoy, if you could cover the weapon aspect of the mission, I'll go over the location and the rest of the plan," Lucero prompted, yanking Poppy out of her stupor.

She dragged her gaze away from Sam to look at the CIA agent. "Of course." Taking a deep breath, she picked up the remote for the projector and focused on the screen. "The image we're looking at is the warhead for a Hwasong-14 intercontinental ballistic missile—an ICBM." She flipped to the next slide, trying to forget who was sitting at the table a mere few feet away. "If the surveillance evidence is to be believed, this is the weapon that Colonel Kam is going to be selling to the Alatas brothers. Based on my review of the drawings and schematics, the warhead is a Teller-Ulam type device with a traditional primary/secondary design and a weight of approximately three hundred twenty kilograms. If that weight holds true, then the North Koreans have achieved warhead miniaturization to a degree that would allow their ICBM reentry vehicles to reach American soil."

There was a murmur of conversation around the table as Sam and his Teammates discussed that possibility.

"More concerning than the weight of the warhead is the appearance of certain components such as the deuterium/tritium containment bottle that you see in this picture here," she added, flipping to the next slide. "That confirms we're dealing with a thermonuclear bomb, also known as a hydrogen bomb. That puts the yield at two hundred fifty kilotons best case, possibly even in the megaton range."

Poppy went through a few more slides, adding details she thought might be critical to their mission, such as safety concerns, background radiation levels, and how large and heavy the warhead shipping container might be. Several of the SEALs asked questions, including Chasen, Wes, and Lane, but fortunately, Sam didn't say a word. Poppy was thankful for that.

Lucero took over after she was done, and Poppy slipped off to the side of the room where she sat down with Nyla. From the look on her friend's face, it was obvious Nyla had figured out that Sam was one of the SEALs in attendance. Poppy shook her head, whispering, "Later."

"We don't have a firm answer on when the weapon exchange is going down," Lucero said, taking over the briefing and motioning to a slide that popped up on the screen. The image showed some rocky terrain, heavily overgrown with brush in places that bare rock was showing through. "But based on the audible intel your Team was able to collect, we've confirmed the deal will go down on Morotai Island, which is part of the North Maluku chain in Indonesia."

Lucero spent some time going over photos of the village where the exchange was supposed to take place, as well as the road network leading through the mountains around the town that would get them back to the coast.

Chasen frowned. "Why are we spending so much time covering the island's road network?"

"Because your mission has changed," Lucero said. "While keeping the Alatas brothers from getting their hands on the weapon is clearly key, national leadership has decided that gaining possession of the nuke for exploitation is a priority.

And since it weighs in excess of seven hundred pounds, carrying it out of there is obviously out of the question. Those roads through the mountains will be your only escape route. Memorizing them will be critical to mission success."

The meeting wrapped up shortly after that since nothing could be done until they had a better idea of when the deal on Morotai would be happening. Lucero said they had people working on it, warning Sam and his Teammates to stay on alert.

Poppy and Nyla nearly made it to the door when she heard Sam call her name. She stopped in her tracks, letting out a sigh.

"Want me to stay?" Nyla asked softly.

She shook her head. "No, that's okay. I'll be fine."

Nyla hesitated, but then nodded and left the room, but not before giving Sam a glare.

"So, you're an expert on foreign nuclear weapons now?" Sam asked when they were alone. "Are you even a professor at all or was that a lie, too?"

"I actually do teach math and physics at the college," she said, her voice as emotionless as Sam's even though her stomach was churning like a washing machine. "It's a necessary part of my cover here, which is okay, because I happen to enjoy it as well. The fact that I'm also an expert in foreign nuclear weapon design is no more a lie than the fact that you never mentioned you'd been on Kepulauan Nenusa conducting surveillance for the CIA, or the follow-up mission to Madura."

"I couldn't tell you about that stuff," he said. "Everything I do in the SEALs is classified. You don't have the clearance for me to tell you."

Poppy folded her arms and snorted. "Trust me, you don't want to start a game of *you show me your clearance, I'll show you mine.* I think you might be disappointed. Regardless, your reasons for not telling me about Indonesia is the same reason I couldn't tell you about the work I do here—clearance and need-to-know. I've never lied to you."

Sam regarded her for a long moment, his expression impossible to read. Then he shook his head. "I don't really know you at all, do I?"

With that, he turned and strode out of the room.

While Poppy hadn't been expecting an apology, she thought Sam would at least be willing to accept that he'd been jumping to conclusions. But she supposed that was too much to ask for.

As pain tore through her heart at that knowledge, she found herself gasping for breath. She would have thought she was past hurting anymore. But she was wrong.

Sam ignored the knock on his door. Since moving out of the dorms, the only people who showed up at his door were his Teammates, takeout delivery people, or neighborhood kids trying to get him to buy candy for their school fund raisers. And Poppy, of course. His Teammates would have texted before coming over, he'd already bought more candy than he could eat in a year, and there was no way in hell it was Poppy.

Poppy was never going to knock on his door again.

Therefore, there was no reason to answer it.

Another knock, louder this time.

Sam didn't move from the couch where he'd been sitting playing video games for the past hour. Whoever the hell was out there would go away sooner or later.

He was fully aware that he was sulking. But

seeing Poppy earlier today had hit him like a punch in the gut, ripping the air from his lungs and reminding him again how difficult it was going to be to get over her.

He hadn't thought too much about it when Chasen had called that morning and told Sam to wear civvies to work, but he'd gotten a little concerned when the van they'd all loaded into had turned into the parking lot of San Diego Mesa College. That concern had turned into full-blown panic when they'd pulled into the parking lot behind the campus's math and physics building.

As they walked through the maze-like hallways to a heavy unmarked door with a key card reader to one side, then were escorted by an armed guard, past more security checkpoints than they had at the Imperial Beach Complex on Coronado, and finally, to a fancy conference room where Lucero had been waiting. Sam had relaxed a little.

Then Poppy had walked in.

To say his Teammates were shocked to see her was putting it mildly. Hell, Sam thought he might actually pass out. Dalton had looked nearly as bad. Then his former girlfriend had started talking, making casual reference to North Korea

ICBM nomenclatures, detailed nuclear warhead designs, and possible TNT equivalent yields. His head began to spin when she'd started going on about warhead miniaturization relative to missile range and deuterium/tritium containment bottles. He'd known she was smart, but that was a whole different level. It was like he'd never met the real Poppy at all.

Things had only gotten worse after the briefing, when he'd confronted her about this new set of lies and deception. Only for her to point out that everything between them had been a lie and a deception. He'd walked out then, unwilling to face the truth of her statement.

The ding of a notification on his phone interrupted his thoughts and he glanced down at his cell to see a text from Lane, asking if he wanted pizza.

I'll never turn down pizza, he wrote back.

Good to hear since we've been standing outside your damn door for the past fifteen minutes, was Lane's reply.

Tossing the game controller on the table, Sam got up and walked around the boxes he still hadn't unpacked to the door, knowing he was being played even as he opened the door. When he'd refused to answer their knock, his buddies had gone with the old pizza trick.

To their credit, Lane and the guys *had* sprung for pizza, so at least he hadn't been completely played. On the downside, Dalton was with Lane and Wes. *Great.* He and Dalton hadn't said a word to each other since their fight and Sam wasn't sure when they would. But at least Dalton's bruises looked worse than his. That was something at least.

"You still haven't unpacked?" Wes asked, shoving some of the boxes aside with his foot to make room around the couch and the other chairs in the living room. "What are you, a slob?"

Sam shrugged, flipping open the first pizza box on the stack Lane had dropped on his coffee table, dragging out a slice of pepperoni. "I still haven't decided if I'm staying. It was awkward enough breaking up with Poppy. Now that I know she's working with the CIA, it's even weirder. I can't imagine having to bump into her on a regular basis."

Nobody said anything, which kind of surprised him. His friends were never at a loss for words. Instead, Dalton walked into the kitchen and came out a few seconds later with a six pack of beer. He popped the top on one, then helped himself to a slice of the pizza.

After they finished the first pizza in silence, Lane opened the second box. This one was sausage with extra cheese. Sam could definitely work with that.

"I was wrong about Poppy," Dalton said, tossing the remains of his most recent slice of pizza into the open box before heading for a fresh one. "She's obviously not a stripper."

Sam stared at the piece of crust lying in the box, thinking about whether he should punch Dalton again. He hated people who wasted the best part of the pizza. He also didn't think much of people who threw their cootie-covered leftovers back in the box, like he thought someone else was going to eat it for him.

"Thanks for that brilliant friggin' observation since I doubt the rest of us would have picked up on that," Sam drawled. "You know, considering the fact that she just delivered a classified briefing for the CIA, using words I imagine you had to look up after the fact and all."

Lane and Wes tensed, like they were both ready to jump up and get between him and Dalton if things turned into a fight again. That effectively confirmed that their sole purpose in coming over here was to stop that from happening. Which meant Dalton must want to talk to Sam about Poppy.

Goody.

"I'm just saying that I was wrong," Dalton repeated slowly. "Maybe it's time you consider that you were wrong, too."

That rather introspective segue definitely caught Sam off guard. "Wrong about what, punching you in the face? Because you can trust me on this, I've never felt better about punching someone than I did you."

Dalton chuckled. "No, you punching me was legit. I should never have said what I did about Poppy, even if I thought it was true at the time. What I'm trying to say is that maybe you were wrong about giving up on her."

Sam wasn't sure what to say. He'd assumed Chasen had told Dalton to talk to him in an effort to patch up the frayed team dynamic that had existed since their brawl. He definitely hadn't expected Dalton to suggest that Sam try and get back together with Poppy.

He had to fight the sudden urge to laugh. "I didn't give up on her. Our relationship imploded because Poppy kept a secret from me."

Dalton let out a snort even as Lane and Wes started in on the third pizza.

"What secret?" Dalton demanded, tossing another piece of crust in the box. "You can't be upset at the fact that she didn't tell you about her real job."

"No," Sam snapped. "I don't care about that. It's hard to complain about Poppy keeping her real job a secret when I did the same thing."

"Then what's the problem?" Dalton asked, actually looking curious, if not a little confused. "Poppy got pissed that you lied about being a SEAL and you got pissed about her lying about being a covert nuclear weapons expert. You both say you're sorry, then get back to being happy. Because trust me, everyone on the Team knows you were happy as hell before this all blew up."

Sam was silent for a moment. Dalton made it sound so easy. "How the hell am I supposed to get back to being happy when all I can think about when I look at Poppy is that she slept with you?"

Dalton frowned. "Look, you probably already

his head on the back of the couch and staring up at the popcorn ceiling as if there might be an answer to his dilemma there. "And that I'm a total jackass who messed up royally. How am I supposed to fix it? I have no idea what to say to Poppy, *if* I can even get her to listen to me."

"I don't know much about women," Lane said, opening up the fourth and last box of pizza. "Actually, it's safe to say I know nothing about women. But even speaking from a place of ignorance, I think you need to start with an apology. Not a generic, *my-bad* type of apology either. I'm talking some serious, on-your-knees, groveling kind of apology."

"You should bring her flowers," Wes added. "Lots of flowers. Women like flowers. Well, Kyla does anyway. Maybe a stuffed animal, too. You can even get a stuffed donkey and use it as part of your apology. You know, hold it out to her and say, *Sorry I was an ass.*"

"I'm not sure Poppy is a stuffed animal kind of woman," Dalton said. "Or that she'd appreciate your juvenile pun." He looked at Sam. "Maybe you should bring her something a math nerd would fawn over, like a graphing calculator."

Sam stared at his Teammates, waiting for them to say more. When they didn't, he let out a sigh. "That's the best you guys have, grovel and bring flowers, a stuffed donkey, or a graphing calculator? No actual tips on what I should say or how I'm going to keep her from slamming the door in my face the moment she sees me?"

Dalton shook his head while Lane and Wes grabbed more pizza.

"Hey, we came here to help you to see the error of your ways, so you could hopefully get back together with Poppy," Dalton pointed out. "You dug this hole for yourself, so you're going to need to find a way to climb out of it. But if you want some serious advice, maybe you might want to think about being honest with her. Tell her why you were such an ass and that you want to start over. It might be the only approach that will work."

Sam knew Dalton was right, but the idea of knocking on Poppy's door and laying it all on the line like that scared the hell out of him. Right now, he didn't even know how to start the conversation.

He was still trying to come up with something when the last of the pizza disappeared, and with it, so did his friends. Sam was still wrapped up in his own head, but that didn't stop him from reaching out to stop Dalton before he left.

"Hey, I just wanted to say thanks for coming over and setting me straight on this. I know you didn't have to after what happened between us in Indonesia."

Dalton grinned. "You're right. I didn't. But no matter how badly you screw up or how many times you punch me, you're still my brother and I'm always going to be there for you. Just don't mess up this chance with Poppy, okay?"

Sam watched his buddies walk away, then gazed across the hall at Poppy's door, wondering how the hell he was ever going to pull off an apology.

CHAPTER
Eleven

THE MOMENT SHE HEARD THE KNOCK AT HER DOOR, Poppy knew it was Nyla. Ever since the SEAL Team briefing two days ago, her friend had been checking on her every few hours, like she was afraid Poppy was going to have a complete and total meltdown. Which was crazy—and unfortunately—closer to the truth than Poppy wanted to admit. She'd been miserable since she and Sam had broken up and the confrontation in *The Cave* had only made it worse. She knew she needed to let it go, that she shouldn't let some jackass guy get to her, and that she shouldn't keep crying over him.

She'd failed miserably at all three of those things. And Nyla knew it.

Even though Poppy was sure it was her friend,

she still checked the peephole. A lifetime of living in a big city had ingrained it into her. When she caught sight of Sam standing in the hallway, she froze, her head going into deep power save mode.

404 Error...Page Not Found.

It took another knock on the door to jar her back to the real world. Poppy seriously considered ignoring Sam and running back to the couch to hide. That's pretty much what she'd been doing for the past two days anyway. Checking the hallway and stairwell before leaving her apartment, then sneaking around and doing anything she could to avoid running into him. Hell, last night she'd purposely worked until nine o'clock simply so she wouldn't have to see him.

"Poppy, I need to talk to you," Sam said softly, his deep voice vibrating through the wood door. "Tell you something I should have told you before all this went so wrong. Please, if there was ever anything between us, give me a chance to say this one thing. If you don't like what I have to say, I promise I'll never bother you again."

Poppy knew she should avoid the drama surely waiting on the other side of the door, but the pain and sorrow in Sam's voice tore at her. She also had to admit, she was curious about what he had to say.

Praying she wasn't making a mistake—a horrible mistake—that would only end up causing her more pain, she slowly flipped the lock on the door and opened it. Sam stood there with his hands behind his back, wearing faded jeans and a soft button-down left casually untucked at the bottom. Even though it had been less than two days since she'd seen him—thirty-two hours and eighteen minutes to be precise—he still took her breath away. He might look like he hadn't slept in days and had more than his usual amount of scruff, but heaven help her, he looked good.

"What are you doing here, Sam?" Poppy asked, needing to say something so she wouldn't blurt out how much she'd missed him.

The frustrating, yet admittedly hunky, SEAL didn't say anything. Instead, he brought out both hands from behind his back. In one, he held a bouquet of red poppies, and in the other, a colorful large plushie, almost completely square in shape. It only took her a second or two to figure out what she was looking at, and when she did, it took everything Poppy had to not launch herself at him and hug him senseless.

"Where did you find a stuffed Rubik's Cube?" she asked, reaching out to take both the flowers and the plushie from his hands, moving aside to let him into the apartment. He'd brought her a stuffed Rubik's Cube. She had to let him in, right?

"There's pretty much nothing you can't find online," he said, stepping inside and letting the door close behind him. "I thought I should bring some kind of peace offering so you'd give me enough time to apologize, and since we first met over a Rubik's cube, I figured it might earn me a few brownie points."

Poppy turned to place the flowers on the coffee table in the living room, so Sam wouldn't see her startled reaction. She'd hoped the conversation might go this way, but truthfully, she hadn't thought it would.

"Is that why you came here tonight?" she asked, her gaze still on the flowers. "To apologize?"

"Yes," he said. "For everything."

"*Everything*?" she repeated, turning back to face him, the plushie clutched possessively in her hands. "Apologizing for *everything* seems kind of vague. If you're sincere about wanting to apologize, it might be better if you tell me exactly what you're apologizing for."

Poppy expected some kind of push back at that, but Sam nodded. He moved further into the living room, but still left a lot of space between them.

"I'm willing to do that if you're willing to listen. Considering how badly I screwed up, it might take a while."

She moved over to the couch and sat down, crisscrossing her legs and holding the soft, squishy cube in her lap. "I don't have any plans for the evening."

Sam sat in one of the chairs off to the side of the couch instead of joining her. For some stupid reason, that hurt. But Poppy pushed the pain down, taking a deep breath and waiting for him to start.

"The bruises you saw on my face when I got back from that mission to Madura Island weren't from getting into it with some bad guys," Sam said, his gaze fixed on the floor. "I got them in a fight with Dalton. We got into it with him when he called you a stripper and said you slept with him because he was a SEAL."

Poppy frowned. People wondered why she liked math so much. It was because men were stupid for the most part. "You got in a fight with a Teammate on a mission because he called me names?"

With the scruff, it was hard to know for sure, but Poppy thought Sam might be blushing a little. It was adorable!

"Yeah. I know that's juvenile," he admitted. "But I was already on edge after the way we'd left things when I had to leave the cookout so suddenly and you'd found out that I was a SEAL, having all those questions I had no time to answer. I couldn't help thinking I'd blown any chance I had with you, and then Dalton implied that I didn't know you at all, that you were just playing me. I just...lost it. If Chasen and the other guys hadn't showed up, we probably would have killed each other."

She blinked. "Seriously?" They had somehow gotten off track as far as Sam's apology, but she wanted to know what had truly happened on the mission. There was something more going on than Sam being offended on her behalf. "Why would you get into a fight over that? There had to be more to it than you wanting to stand up for my honor. For all you knew, he was right about me."

Sam didn't answer right away, but from the look on his face, it was obvious she'd stumbled on something. Then his expression relaxed, as if he'd come to a decision.

"I slugged Dalton because I was jealous, okay?" he said, the words coming out in a jumble. "I couldn't handle knowing that a buddy of mine had been with you. Yeah, it's petty, cave-mannish, and pretentious considering I'd known you for barely two weeks, yet there it is. The thought that Dalton of all people had slept with you hurt like hell and I took it out on him. Then, when I got back, I took it out on you. And that's the part I need to apologize for. I had no right to get jealous. Who you were with before we met is none of my business. And you obviously had no idea Dalton and I knew each other. But I was jealous and it made me act like a friggin' jackass. And for that—as well as everything I said to you because of it—I'm sorry."

Poppy had never expected this level of honesty when the conversation had started. As apologies went, she had to admit, this one was pretty awesome. But his explanation did leave her with more than a few questions.

"Apology accepted," she said. "But you know you have absolutely nothing to be jealous about, right? What happened between me and Dalton wasn't anything real. Nothing like what we had."

Sam took a deep breath, then let it out. "I know that now. It took some time—and a little browbeating from Dalton and the other guys—for me to get there. In hindsight, I realize that my reaction to you sleeping with Dalton had more to do with me than you."

"What do you mean?" Poppy asked.

She was genuinely confused now. But then again, she never understood men at the best of times. She glanced down at the plush Rubik's Cube in her hands, wondering why no one had come up with a math algorithm to solve men yet.

"My conversation with Dalton and the other guys led to a bit of self-reflection, so I asked myself why I got so upset when I found out the two of you had been together." Sam shrugged. "Long story short, it's possible I'm carrying a bit of baggage due to being one of the newest members of the same SEAL Team my dad led for years. It's filled with guys who have known me since I was a kid and I think some of them still see me that way, no matter how many missions I go on. It's made me kind of sensitive to criticism from them. So, when I finally stumbled over something amazing that's all mine, only to discover you have a previous history with someone else on the Team, it triggered an insecurity I never realized I had."

Silence filled the living room, giving Poppy time to think over everything Sam had said. And there had definitely been a lot. But she could easily understand where he was coming from.

"Look, I don't expect you to be okay with any of this," Sam said before she could speak. "I only wanted you to understand where my head was in all this crap and tell you sincerely how sorry I am for everything I said. I've done that, so there's no reason for me to hang around any longer."

He started to stand, but Poppy quickly waved him back down. "Stay. Please. You may have gotten everything off your chest, but there are a few things I'd like to say."

Sam looked confused, but he sat back down.

"While I'll agree wholeheartedly that you were a jackass and should probably be apologizing for the next month, I also have a few insecurities of my own that almost certainly added some drama to the situation," she began.

"Okay," he said.

"You remember how tense I got when you confronted me about the whole Dalton thing, right? The way I sort of went on the offensive the second you started in on me about it?" When Sam nodded, she kept going. "I know I already told you some of this, but I went out with lots of men who wanted me for my face or my body, but then bailed the second I opened my mouth and said something... smart. I mean, it happened to me on the reg since I was a teenager. Over and over, dozens of times. Until I started to hate the real me. Sometimes, I wished I really was that dumb bimbo Dalton found so attractive. It messed with my head. Until you showed up and I started thinking I'd found the man I'd always been waiting for."

"And then I came out and pretty much called you a bimbo, then walked away," Sam said quietly.

She nodded. "Yeah. It was like my worst nightmare coming true. So, when you left, I was so devastated, I didn't try and stop you. My fear of never being good enough for anyone cost me the only man I'd ever felt anything for."

If she'd thought the room had been quiet after Sam's confession, it was so silent now, she could have heard a pin drop.

"Like you'd said earlier, I don't expect you to be okay with any of this," she told him softly. "I only wanted you to understand why I behaved the way I did. So, this is me apologizing for the role I played in everything falling apart."

Setting the plush Rubik's Cube on the couch beside her, she stood. Sam got to his feet, too.

"So, what do we do now?" she asked. "Do you think we can get past this?"

"That depends on you and what you want," he said. "Finding a way to make this work is why I showed up at your door again in the first place, but it's ultimately up to you."

"I want that, too." She took one step, then another, closing the distance between them. "But how do we do that?"

"Maybe it's as simple as being willing to start over?" he said, reaching out to take her hand in his big one.

She smiled up at him, not sure if it would be

162 | PAIGE TYLER

that easy, but willing to try to get back what she'd lost.

"Hi, I'm Poppy McCoy," she said. "I occasionally teach math and physics at San Diego Mesa College when I'm not evaluating foreign nuclear weapon designs for a variety of covert organizations."

Sam grinned down at her, and it felt like the sun coming out after a very long storm. "It's nice to meet you, Poppy. I'm Sam Travers, Navy SEAL, and I frequently find myself working for a variety of those organizations. Small world, huh?"

She was about to agree with him in regards to the world definitely being small when his head dipped down and captured her mouth with his.

Poppy moaned softly as Sam's strong arms came around her, providing that sense of warmth and protection she only now realized how much she'd missed. Slipping her hand into the short hair along the back of his head, she tugged his mouth down harder, losing herself in the sensation of his taste.

After a moment, she broke away, making a decision. Seeing the questioning look in his eyes, she trailed one hand along his arm until her fingers latched with his. Then she tugged, turning to head toward her bedroom at the same time.

Sam didn't resist.

When they reached her room, the only light she turned on was the small lamp on her bedside table. Then she turned to Sam, gazing up at him as she slowly unbuttoned his shirt. Neither one of them said a word as she slid the material over his broad shoulders, her fingers tracing over the ridges of his well-defined muscles.

The rest of their clothes came off as slowly, the only sound that of fabric hitting the floor. When they were both completely naked, Poppy stood there looking at Sam in the dim glow of the lamp. He looked so perfect like this. Like something out of a dream. Her dreams for sure.

They kissed again, her breasts pressing against his powerful chest, his hard shaft firm against her belly. She could stay like this forever and be supremely happy.

But soon enough, both of them were pawing at the condom packaging, Sam tearing the foil as Poppy pulled out the latex and carefully rolled it down his achingly hard erection. Then she was nudging him back on the bed and climbing on top

of him, slowly easing herself down on him and letting out audible sighs at the pleasurable sensation
of him sliding in deep. She leaned forward, kissing him gently even as she rode him. There was no
urgency to their movements, only a slow appreciation of each other's company.

Poppy felt a tear slid down her cheek and
moved her head to the side to let her shoulder intercept its fall. She didn't want him to think that
she was unhappy, when she was, in fact, the very
furthest from that. The moment was so perfect it
made her cry.

They continued to move, Sam's hands sliding up and down her back, warm and comforting.
After they'd established a rhythm both of them enjoyed, one of his hands found a permanent position on her butt, the other in her hair. He didn't
quite control her movements, but he definitely
helped her do some of the work.

She'd never had sex where the whole goal
seemed to be enjoying each other rather than
chasing an orgasm. But she had to admit, it was
glorious.

Time sort of lost meaning as they continued to
make love, but then the grinding of her clit against

the base of his cock started the tingling deep inside her that had always presaged a climax. Still,
Poppy kept the pace tortuously slow, not in any
rush for this to end. Amazingly, Sam seemed good
with keeping everything chill, too.

The moment reminded Poppy of being on
a gigantic roller coaster, tension building as she
climbed until she thought there was no way she
could go any higher, at least without running out
of oxygen. And then there was that breathtaking
second when she was balanced right there on the
edge, almost sliding back, almost tipping forward.
Then she was falling, air rushing up to meet her as
she completely went into a free fall.

The big drop stole her breath, vision, and
voice. Then she was keening and twisting atop
him, his strong hands keeping her in place, driving
him deeper inside her. Poppy thought she might
fly off into space right then, and possibly would
have, if it wasn't for Sam's arms around her.

His mouth was right next to her ear when he
let loose inside her, his grunts moving her soul as
much as the pleasure of her climax did. She said
the words then, telling him she loved him. But between his groans and her wrung-out voice, she

doubted he heard. But it was true nonetheless. She loved him. As impossible as that seemed.

Sam got the sheet and blanket around them somehow, and Poppy lay there, content to simply be with him for now. But tomorrow, first thing, she'd repeat the words he hadn't heard.

Then his cell phone rang.

CHAPTER
Twelve

"WE NEED TO HURRY," CHASEN TOLD THE DRIVER as Sam and the rest of his Teammates climbed into the shuttle bus parked in front of the headquarters building. "The plane is scheduled to leave from the North Island Airfield in fifteen minutes."

The driver, who had to be pissed about taking them to the airfield after their mission briefing at 0300 hours, didn't complain. He merely nodded and closed the doors, hitting the gas before most of them had even gotten seated.

"So, what happened with you and Poppy?" Lane asked, turning around in the seat to look at Sam. "Did you give her flowers and a stuffed toy when you showed up to grovel?"

Dalton, Wes, and everyone else in the bus all

turned to look his way, blatantly interested in his answer. Sam was glad it was dark so they couldn't see his face.

"Yeah, I went to talk to her. And yes, I brought flowers and a plushie when I showed up to grovel." He grinned. "She forgave me for being a jackass and we're going to try and make it work."

His Teammates cheered. Wes even leaned forward to slap him on the shoulder, congratulating him like he'd won the lottery. Which he supposed, in a way, he had.

Fortunately, there were no more questions, and Sam leaned back in the seat, relaxing as much as he could during the short trip to the airfield. It was impossible not thinking about Poppy and the night they'd shared. Yes, it had been ruined by that call to come in for a mission, but for that one moment in time as he'd held her close, everything had been right in the world. He had her back, and he wasn't going to blow it this time.

There had been some panic on Poppy's part when he told her that he had to go on a mission, but overall, she'd handled it well. He'd gotten dressed and they'd kissed. *Really* kissed. Then he'd headed out, promising he'd be careful and call her as soon as he was able.

Now, he and his Teammates were heading back to Indonesia with a specific meeting time for the weapon exchange on Morotai Island and a directive to not only stop the weapons deal but also recover the nuke so it could be exploited for every little piece of intelligence that could be gleaned from it. Sam knew Poppy would play a major role in that part of the operation.

Assuming he and his buddies were able to get the damn weapon out of the bad guy's hands and back to the US in one piece.

Closing his eyes, Sam replayed every second of the kiss he'd shared with Poppy, promising himself he'd forever savor the memory like it was the most precious thing in the world to him. Right up until the moment he saw her again. Then he'd replace the memories of that kiss with memories of the next perfect kiss.

It turned out that closing his eyes wasn't a good idea, since he was nearly asleep by the time they reached the small unmarked cargo plane waiting out on the end of the runway. If Lane hadn't whacked him on the shoulder, Sam might have slept right through the stop.

Sam was the last one off the shuttle bus, the driver nearly catching his backpack in the doors as he slammed them closed and spun the vehicle around to leave. He stood there for a second, watching the bus drive away, turning when he heard the engines of the plane spinning up.

Then he saw the person standing at the bottom of the stairs, and all rational thoughts about leaving on time and rude bus drivers fell right out of his head.

"Poppy? How the hell did you get them to let you come here to see me off?" he whisper-shouted, moving quickly across the flight line to where she was standing. "Not that I'm complaining."

Two things occurred to him as he started to hug Poppy. The extremely serious expression on her face and the black tactical backpack resting against one of her legs. Like she was planning to go somewhere with it.

"What's going on?" he asked slowly, a funny feeling building in his stomach.

"I'm not here to see you off, though I would have if that had been an option," she said, her voice tinged with what he thought might be worry. "I'm going with you on the mission. I got the call about ten minutes after you left. Recovering the weapon is a top priority, but both the CIA and the Navy wanted the thing inspected before you brought it back in case it's fake or has been booby trapped. I had no idea they were considering having me come, but I'm their best choice for something like this."

Sam found himself unable to breathe. *What the hell was Poppy saying?* "You can't come on the mission. It's too dangerous. I'm not letting you come!"

He realized his error about half a second before a furious expression appeared on Poppy's face. Crap, she looked ready to murder him. But before she could unload on him, a figure appeared at the top of the plane's stairs, looking down at them with a frown.

"Is there a problem here, Petty Officer Travers?" Lucero asked, coming down several of the steps until he was closer. "Before you answer that, let me point out that I have seven other SEALs already seated in the plane and ready to go, but only one expert on foreign nuclear weapons. So, if there is a problem, I'd have no issue leaving your ass out here on the runway as we fly away."

With that, Lucero turned and walked back up the steps and into the plane, leaving Sam standing there with a very annoyed Poppy.

"This is my job, Sam. Now, don't try and hover over me on the mission." She picked up her backpack and slung it over her shoulder. "That will just get both of us killed. You do your thing and I'll do mine."

The engines droned louder, making further conversation impossible, even if Sam had known what to say. Finally, not having any other choice, he hitched his own backpack a little higher on his shoulder and headed up the steps after her. This mission had just gotten a whole lot harder. Hopefully, it wouldn't tear apart his recently repaired relationship with Poppy...maybe permanently this time.

CHAPTER
Thirteen

'M ON AN ACTUAL SUBMARINE!

Poppy practically squealed as she, Sam, and his fellow SEALs stood in the extremely cramped space beneath the forward hatch, listening as Lucero and Chasen once again went over the plan they'd been putting together for the past five hours. Poppy tried to pay attention, figuring the stuff was important, but it was hard to hear anything with her heart thumping a hundred miles an hour. It didn't help that the only light in the space were a few dim red bulbs along the ceiling, creating one hell of a somber mood.

This entire trip had been like one of those scenes from *Indiana Jones*, where they show you a map of the world with a plane slowly moving across it trailing a dotted red line so the audience can see where you've been and where you're going.

Except in this case, there had been one plane to take them to Oahu, and another one to Batam. Then they'd ridden in a helicopter out to a rather innocent looking cargo ship in the middle of nowhere, which in turn had passed them off to the sub they were currently riding in. All in all, she'd experienced more excitement in the past twenty hours or so than she had in her entire life.

"The captain is concerned about the number of surface ships moving in this area," Lucero said softly, pointing out something on the map laid out on the table in front of them. "So, when that hatch opens, your Team is going to need to move fast. All of you have to be in your boats and gone in less than three minutes."

Poppy eyed the narrow ladder leading up to the hatch, then down to the heavy tactical gear and boots she was wearing, the reality of exactly how real this situation was hitting her. How the hell was she supposed to move fast up a ladder, wearing all this crap?

The black uniform and boots were bad enough, but the Kevlar body armor was insane. It

weighed a ton and made her feel like a claustro-
phobic turtle. She'd tried to talk the guys out of
having to wear it, claiming she wasn't going into
this operation to fight, but that had only earned
her a glare from Sam.

"Wear it or don't go," Lucero said, ending the
argument, such as it was.

Of course, the CIA didn't care about having
to wear all the stuff since he wasn't going on the
mission with them.

There was a little voice in Poppy's head telling her she'd made a serious mistake coming, that
there was no way in hell she could do this. She was
only going to get herself killed. But then reason
took over and she forced herself to calm down. She
was here now. There was no going back.

When Lucero disappeared into some other
part of the submarine, Poppy watched as Sam
and his Teammates finished making last minutes checks of their weapons and other equipment.
She checked her own backpack, making sure everything she needed was still in there and hadn't
shaken loose during the trip. Then Sam came over
and started streaking black grease paint across
the skin of her cheeks, nose, and chin. They hadn't

talked much since the argument on the runway, but she knew in her heart that he'd have her back throughout this mission. It was comforting beyond belief.

"This will tone down the high points on your face, keep light from reflecting off your skin, and help you blend into the background," Sam explained as he worked, his gaze intent. "Just make sure you keep your hair under the helmet. Hair as blond as yours will glow like neon in the dark."

She started to say thanks, but then the red lights overhead started flicking and everyone started moving—fast.

Poppy wasn't aware she was climbing the ladder until water started splashing on her face. She froze, sure they'd opened the hatch while they were still underwater, but Sam's tap on her boot kept her moving. A few moments later, she realized that the water was runoff coming from the top of the sub.

Okay, so they weren't all going to drown. At least not yet anyway.

Once on deck, Poppy mostly stayed out of the way as Sam and the guys got the little—emphasis on *little*—rubber Zodiac boats out of the deck shelter and into the water. Thankfully, the waves weren't too rough and she was able to make it into one of the two boats without falling in the water. She considered that a positive sign.

She ended up in a boat with Sam, Wes, Lane, and Dalton, which left Chasen, Noah, Nash, and Holden in the other. No one said a word the whole time they were loading up the boats, but she couldn't imagine it was coincidence she was with Sam.

The engines on the boats were so whisper quiet that Poppy could barely hear them. Mimicking the others in the boat, she straddled the inflated rubber pontoon on one side, laying down on it and making herself as small as possible while holding on tight. Behind them, the submarine disappeared silently back into the depths like it had never been there.

It was kind of creepy.

The other boat moved off into the darkness, so far away that Poppy couldn't see it. She flipped down the night vision goggles she'd been given, but even with the training Sam and Lane had given her on the flight over, it was still disorienting to use them. She had no clue how Dalton—who was steering the boat—knew where he was going.

If it wasn't for the rapid beating of her heart and the occasional slash of sea spray coming up to douse her face, Poppy probably would have fallen asleep because the soft droning of the engine was surprisingly relaxing. But far faster than she would have imagined, she saw the darker blur of land ahead of them, and she knew they'd arrived on Morotai Island. The mission was about to start, whether she was ready or not.

Dalton timed their approach to the beach perfectly, bringing them in between two large waves. The boat barely tipped up a little in the back, and then they were sliding up the sandy beach, Dalton yanking the motor up so the propellers wouldn't hit the sand.

Sam had her out of the boat before they had even stopped moving. Then she pretty much got out of the way again as he and the guys lifted the boat and ran up the beach with it. They moved faster with a boat full of gear than she did empty-handed.

They slid the boat under the brush and trees growing along the top of the beach. Looking around, she saw that Chasen's group was hiding their boat in similar fashion further down the beach. Gear was unloaded and packs were strapped on quickly, everything being done without a single sound being made. She watched in awe as Sam and his Teammates checked and double-checked each other's packs and gear.

Sam came over and checked her pack, making sure the straps along the shoulders and the one around her hips were snug. "What's in here? It's heavier than I thought you'd carry."

"A nuke first-aid kit," she said softly. "In case things go wrong and I have to work on the weapon."

From the look on Sam's face, it was clear he didn't like the sound of that. A quick glance around at the other guys confirmed they weren't so thrilled either. Then again, if she had to keep the nuke from going full yield and taking out this entire island, she imagined they'd be doing cartwheels.

Sam and his Teammates started moving inland without a word. One second they were all standing there, the next they were running through the jungle. Everyone spread out, and she did her best to stay close to Sam. Poppy had no doubt that if she got separated from him and the other SEALs, she'd be wandering around here all night. She breathed a silent prayer of thanks that she was an avid runner. Even so, jogging through the thick brush while wearing a heavy pack and body armor was drastically different than anything she'd ever done. Ten minutes in and she was already exhausted.

Every once in a while, Sam or one of the other guys would hold up a single fist and stop in their tracks. Sometimes, they'd kneel down, other times they'd stand there motionless as statues. She never had a clue what was going on, but she did whatever they did.

A few minutes later, the hill they were climbing was so close to being vertical she had to climb hand-over-hand. She was glad it was too dark to know how far off the ground they were. Sam was right behind her, steadying her with his hands if she faltered and keeping her from slipping. It was hard to put into words how grateful she was for his presence.

When they reached the top of the ridge, Poppy could see the dim lights of a village below them. They'd have to climb down more rough terrain to get closer. But even from here, she recognized the village as the one from the planning briefing. Though she had to admit, it had seemed a bit more substantial in the overhead photos.

"I know Lucero covered this during the briefing," she whispered to Sam as she took a gulp from her water bag. "But he doesn't honestly think we're going to be able to bring the nuke back by the same route we came in, right?"

Sam took a drink from his own water bag. "Carrying it out by hand was always the backup to the back-up plan. The primary plan is for us to transport the weapon out using whatever vehicle the bad guys have it in now, taking the road through the mountains to the coast, then south down the coastal highway to the beach where a larger boat will be waiting. That route will take longer and comes with its own problems. Getting through the mountain passes will be hard enough in the dark and there are multiple checkpoints we'll have to get through. There's also the distinct possibility that we'll be chased by whatever is left of the two groups we stole the nuke from, so there's that to look forward to as well."

"That does sound bad," she agreed. "But I still

think that will be better than trying to carry a nuke down that cliff we climbed."

"I'll remind you of that when we're getting shot at later," Sam teased, mouth quirking.

She would have laughed if that didn't sound so scary.

They moved off the ridge and into the village, slipping from building to building. The place was eerily quiet, but Poppy could still hear soft voices coming from some of the tiny houses they passed.

"The locals know something's going down," Wes said from behind her. "And they're all hiding, praying they live through whatever's coming."

Poppy didn't comment as they made their way to the edge of an open area in the center of the village. It was a few hundred feet across, surrounded by one- and two-story wooden structures on all sides. The square was thankfully well-lit, allowing her to push up those ridiculous NVGs. If she didn't think she might need them later, she'd yank them off her helmet and toss them under the nearest porch.

They moved close enough to see what was going on but kept back far enough to stay hidden. Pulling a set of binoculars from her backpack, she scanned the area and was surprised by the number of vehicles scattered around. There were well over a dozen of them, including a large military looking cargo truck. If the nuke was here, it'd be in there.

She swung the binoculars toward the men gathered in the square and recognized Colonel Kam and Major Tae from photos Lucero had shown them on the submarine. The Alatas Brothers were there, too, along with plenty of extra muscle. There had to be at least fifty armed men around the square and every one of them looking tense and ready to shoot someone.

"We wait until the transfer has been made," Chasen said softly over the radio. "I hate to let these rogues from North Korea get away, but it will be easier to recover the nuke if we're only dealing with half the group."

Poppy was clueless about these kinds of tactical situations, but Chasen's plan seemed brilliant to her. Fighting half the people still seemed nearly impossible, but it had to be better than fighting all of them.

She wiggled under a beaten-up porch with Sam and Lane, while Dalton and Wes slipped into the deeper shadows of a corner. In the square

184 | PAIGE TYLER

below, the men were arguing about something. After five minutes of yelling at each other, some of the men from the North Korean contingent moved over to the large cargo truck and dragged out a metal container roughly the size of a coffin.

The eight men holding it weren't small, and yet they still had to work hard to keep from dropping it. *Note to self*, she thought. The back-up plan was now officially canceled. No way in hell were Sam and the other SEALs carrying that thing back over the mountains.

The men placed the container on the ground with a solid thud, then flipped the latches. The tension down there was thick enough to cut with a knife. Maybe they'd get lucky and the two groups would take each other out, then she and the guys could take off with the nuke without having to do anything.

Nah. Things never worked out that easily.

One of the men opened the lid, revealing the missile warhead inside. There was some more conversation, along with some more arguing, then one of the North Koreans came forward and removed a few panels from the side of the warhead.

Poppy used her binoculars to study the

exposed portions of the warhead, then the radiac one of the Alatas brothers waved around near the missile. "That's definitely a live nuclear warhead," she whispered into her microphone. "The background radiation is right in the range I'd expect for a weapon of that size and design."

The Alatas brothers must have thought so, too, since both of them made a motion toward one of the other vehicles near the far edge of the square. A moment later, a man came over carrying a large briefcase. Poppy wondered what the going rate was for a high-yield nuclear warhead these days. Five million? Ten million? Who the hell knew.

"Okay," Chasen's voice came over Poppy's earpiece. "That's our cue to move into position. We go in the second the North Koreans are out of the area."

Sam and Lane immediately started to slip out from under the porch, but Sam stopped before he got too far. He turned back to kiss Poppy, a difficult move under the decrepit porch.

"I want you to stay right here without moving a muscle, no matter what you see or hear," he said. "Can you do that for me?"

Poppy nodded, though she was terrified at the

idea of him getting into a firefight with so many armed men. She only prayed he was as good at his job as she hoped.

Another quick kiss and then Sam disappeared into the darkness with Lane, Wes, and Dalton. She wiggled back further under the porch and took up her binoculars to watch the tail end of the weapon buy.

Poppy watched as the man holding the briefcase opened it. Colonel Kam picked up the black velvet bag inside, then reached into it and came out with a handful of diamonds. Even in the dim light around the village square, the gems glittered like crazy. Kam nodded in satisfaction. A second later, the men who'd carried the box with the warhead into the square put it back on the truck. Kam and his security forces moved away. The Alatas brothers did the same. It looked like the deal was done.

"Okay, it's a go," Chasen whispered into the radio. "Everybody move into final positions. We go on my command."

Poppy's heart pounded so hard, it was all she could seem to hear. Which was why she missed the sound of footsteps beside the porch. She peeked out, her blood going cold when she saw a dozen heavily armed men moving toward the village square. Judging from their mismatched clothing and weaponry, they were aligned with the Alatas brothers, and if she had to guess, she'd say they were moving to intercept Colonel Kam and his soldiers as they left the village.

Crap, the brothers were about to double cross the North Koreans, right as Sam and the other SEALs were moving in to recover the warhead.

Poppy had to warn them.

CHAPTER
Fourteen

S AM MOVED FAST TOWARD THE VILLAGE SQUARE, slipping from hut to house, ready to engage with the Alatas brothers and their men, when the hair on the back of his neck shot up. Something was wrong. He opened his mouth to shout a warning over the radio, but then shooting started on the far side of the village, and he knew it was too late to stop the raid. Chasen's team had already engaged. They were all committed now.

"There's a group of heavily armed men coming at you from my direction," Poppy's distinct voice came over the radio. "They're dressed like the Alatas gang, so I think they're planning to ambush the North Koreans.

Sam heard his Teammates curse over the

radio as gunfire erupted to the left. That was the direction the Korean forces had taken.

"More men are coming. At least ten of them," Poppy said even as Chasen began shouting out orders to change the plan. "But these guys are dressed like the North Koreans. What the hell is going on?"

It was hard getting a word through all the chatter as Sam's Teammates called out warnings to each other. The background noise of gunfire flooded the mics, making it worse.

"I want you to keep your head down," he told Poppy, praying she could hear him. "Don't move no matter what happens!"

Sam rounded the corner of a building at full speed, Lane coming around the other side at the same time. They both arrived in the village square in time to see everything going to hell. The North Koreans, who seconds ago had been leaving the village, had turned and were now attacking in force. It was obvious they had reinforcements who'd been hiding in case everything went to crap. The Alatas brothers and their men were arrayed to the right behind several vehicles with some of the backup Poppy had mentioned.

And stuck in the middle of both sides was Sam's rather small SEAL team—along with a nuclear weapon that probably wouldn't like getting shot.

Sam ducked as bullets tore up the ground around him, rounds coming from both sides of the conflict. He would have laughed if he wasn't so focused on trying to stay alive. This wasn't merely a one-sided double cross. The North Koreans apparently wanted their nuke back while keeping the diamonds. The terrorists wanted their diamonds while keeping the nuke. He guessed there really was no honor among thieves.

Poppy kept calling out warnings, using her hidden observation point on the edge of the village square to let them know when either one of the enemy forces was starting to gather themselves for a charge. Sam never would have thought it, but she was amazingly cool in a firefight.

A few moments later, Sam found himself fighting with Lane and Wes at his back, surrounded on all sides by people trying to kill them as the three of them tried to reach the big military truck and its nuclear cargo. Sam flinched as bullets tore through the canvas tarp stretched over the back of the vehicle, and he prayed the bullets hadn't struck something sensitive.

If the bad guys weren't so interested in killing each other, Sam and his Teammates would have been wiped out long ago. Even so, it still took much longer to reach the center of the village square than it should have. And then, just as they were within reach of the truck and the nuke they were after, Poppy's voice over the radio froze him solid.

"Someone found my hiding place!" she shouted, and Sam could hear the rush of air across the mic that told him Poppy was running for her life. "I'm heading toward the south end of the village...I think. They're behind me."

Sam caught Chasen's eye across the chaotic battlefield. That was all it took.

"Take Wes and Lane and go help her!" Chasen shouted. "The rest of us will get the nuke."

Sam took off running, heading in a direction he prayed would allow him to intercept Poppy's path. Bullets tore up the ground around him, but he kept going, depending on Wes and Lane to cover him as he moved straight across the square. When he reached the first building, he kept going, ignoring common sense that told him to slow down long enough to look around the corner first. No matter how crazy it was, he couldn't slow down. Poppy was out there somewhere, and she was in trouble.

He ran past several more houses, panic setting in as he started thinking that maybe he'd gone the wrong direction and misjudged how fast Poppy could run. Then he heard automatic gunfire ahead of him immediately followed by a feminine scream that was impossible to miss. Sam sprinted around the next corner only to almost get run over by Wes and Lane as all three of them slid to a stop at the sight in front of them.

Major Tae and about a half dozen of his soldiers were firing from the left side of a small playground at Adika Alatas and a bunch of his men who were returning fire from the right.

Poppy was smack in the middle of everything, huddled down behind a rusted merry-go-round as bullets from both sides zipped over her head and the backpack she was still wearing.

Sam's heart froze solid in his chest. The air he so desperately needed in his lungs wouldn't come. Even though his fear for Poppy nearly made him vapor-lock, Sam's feet carried him forward before he even realized he was moving. On automatic pilot, his M4 carbine came up and he started shooting at the people closest to Poppy—Adika Alatas and his men.

Two of them were down before anyone realized Sam and his buddies had shown up for the party. He was less than ten feet away from Poppy's position when a blur of motion made Sam whip his head to the side just in time to see Adika Alatas charging at him at full speed, AK-47 assault weapon blazing away.

Sam didn't have time to get his M4 around. So instead, he threw himself to the ground, rolling as bullets passed by so close, he swore he felt them. Then he was on his feet again, slamming into Adika, taking them both down hard.

His M4 got trapped between his chest and

the other man's hip, and he had no chance to get it free since he was focused entirely on keeping Adika from shooting him. Sam shoved the barrel of Adika's AK away from his face just as it went off. The blast from the muzzle made his ears ring.

Cursing, Sam punched the man as hard as he could, raining down blow after blow while bullets flew all around them. He'd never minded a good brawl, even when automatic weapons were involved, but trying to fight while keeping an eye out for Poppy was nerve-wracking as hell.

Sam glanced her way when Adika slammed his knee into his side, practically caving in his ribs. The force of the blow sent Sam rolling across the ground and his weapon flying. Knowing he was screwed, he got up and lunged toward his M4 lying a few feet away. There was no way he'd reach it before he got shot, but he was damn sure going to try anyway. He only prayed Wes and Lane would get Poppy out of here.

Hitting the ground, Sam grabbed his weapon, twisting his body to swing it around in time. Pain bloomed in his chest as he squeezed the trigger of his carbine and got off a three-round burst in Adika's direction. Then he was flying backwards, every ounce of air in his lungs whooshing out. Shot, it felt like he'd been kicked by a mule.

Sam barely felt it when he landed, which only reinforced the idea that he was in seriously deep crap. He lay there, fighting for air as pain migrated from the center of his chest and out into both arms. His vision went a little dim then. Damn, getting shot hurt.

Suddenly, Poppy was leaning over him, her hands pulling at his tactical vest, face consumed with worry. "Sam, are you okay? Talk to me!"

He gazed up at the woman he loved, abruptly realizing he should have told her that, but also wondering how she could possibly ask such a question. He'd been shot. Didn't she realize he was dying? But before he could say anything, Lane appeared and dragged him upright.

"Come on. We have to go!" his buddy said. "Chasen has cleared the village square and is waiting for us. Stop screwing around!"

Sam couldn't help but look around in confusion, wondering when the hell everyone had decided that getting shot counted as *screwing around*. But then he finally looked down and realized there wasn't any blood on him. His tactical vest was shredded and the ballistic plate underneath looked as if something had exploded in the middle of it. Breathing still seemed like something that other people did right now, too, but he wasn't bleeding. Or dead.

He looked over to see Adika Alatas lying on the ground motionless, three holes drilled through the center of his chest. Apparently, Sam had gotten his shots off in time. And unlike him, Adika hadn't been wearing a vest.

There were several other bodies as well, both from the North Korean contingent and those who'd been with Adika. No sight of Major Tae, though. That wasn't a good sign. Sam had the feeling the man was dangerous as hell.

"You okay?" Poppy asked again, her eyes glistening with tears she was clearly fighting to hold back. "When I saw you fall, I thought you were..."

"I'm all right," he said, pulling her into his arms. "Just got the breath knocked out of me, that's all. I was more worried about you. I'm glad you're okay."

Her hand tightened on his shoulders. "You came for me."

"Always," Sam said simply.

He would have kissed her, but Wes and Lane were looking antsy as hell. Both guys were motioning for him to wrap it up.

"I really want to kiss you right now," he whispered. "But we have to move before Chasen leaves us behind."

Poppy didn't complain, running to keep up with him, holding onto the shoulder straps of her pack to keep it from bouncing too much. Sam considered telling her to dump it but knew she'd never do it. That pack—and the stuff inside it—were part of the reason she'd come on this mission. She couldn't do her job without it.

A lot of gunfire was coming from the center of the village, but by the time they got there, it all but disappeared. Chasen was beside a small pick-up truck, motioning for them to hurry.

"Both groups have retreated, but they'll be back soon enough," Chasen said, pointing Lane toward the passenger seat of the big cargo truck where Dalton was already waiting behind the wheel with the engine running. "And I sure as hell don't want to be here when they do."

Wes took off running toward another small pick-up truck, this one full of bullet holes. Even the windows were shot out. Sam was about to lead Poppy in that direction, but she was already running for the back of the military cargo truck.

"I need to check the nuke and make sure it's still in a safe condition after all the shooting."

The truck was already moving and they had to run to catch up to it. Sam helped Poppy into the back, then hopped in after her. They barely made it in before Dalton stomped on the accelerator and the truck lurched forward. Chasen's vehicle raced ahead of them while Wes and the other guys fell in behind them to protect their six.

"Crap," Poppy said, her voice barely audible over their truck's roaring diesel engine.

Sam spun around to see her staring at the ragged holes that had torn through the canvas along the sides of the cargo bed. It only got worse as he followed her gaze further and saw the matching holes in the side of the nuke.

"Should it be smoking like that?" Sam asked, frowning at the acrid smoke slowly filling the air.

"No." Poppy crawled forward on her hands and knees only to fall over as the truck swerved violently and gunfire echoed around them.

Sam glanced out the back of the truck to see an absolute entourage of bad guys following them.

Shit.

Poppy ignored the shooting and continued over to the weapon on her hands and knees, yanking the backpack off her shoulder as she moved.

"At least one of those bullets hit something in there that didn't like it," she said, reaching into her bag for a small battery-operated drill.

"Is there anything in a nuke that doesn't mind being shot?" Sam asked.

The smoking was getting worse. Maybe they should try and shove the nuke out of the truck before things got out of hand.

Poppy seemed to think about his question for a moment. "Actually, now that I think about it, no. There's nothing inside a nuclear weapon that would take kindly to being shot."

Before Sam could say anything more, she began unscrewing and unbolting covers and panels on the weapon he hadn't even realized were there. He would have helped, but it didn't look like she needed any. Something told him she'd done this before—a lot.

"Could this thing go high order?" he asked worriedly.

"You mean produce a high-yield nuclear blast?" Poppy replied, not taking her eyes off the weapon as she took off another panel, cursing a little as it sizzled in her hands from the heat building up inside the thing. She tossed it aside even as flames began to appear in the nuke. "Most likely not."

He sagged with relief. "That's good."

"Depends on your definition of good," she murmured, still not looking at him. "If the fire reaches the explosives around the pit, the weapon is will start releasing high levels of alpha radiation. If that gets into our lungs...well...let's just say it won't end well for us. If the fire progresses beyond that and gets completely out of hand, the HE could undergo a burn to detonate transfer. It wouldn't create much of a yield—no mushroom cloud or anything—but we'd be dead, and the radiation scatter would make a good portion of this island, as well as the ones downwind, uninhabitable for the next decade or so."

Yeah, that was bad.

"What do we do?" Sam asked, stunned she was so calm. He sure as hell wasn't. And he was a SEAL. Getting shot at didn't bother him but glowing in the dark was not on his list of things he wanted to do in this life.

"We have to strip the warhead down and get enough of the outer skin off to figure out what's going on in there, then put the fire out," she said.

Sam moved over to help and was immediately tossed aside as the truck swerved and the base of the nuke container slid halfway across the back of the cargo bed, only to slide back the other direction as they went around a curve on the mountainous road way too fast, nearly crushing Poppy against the side rails of the vehicle.

"Dalton, slow the hell down!" Sam shouted through the broken back-glass of the cab. "Poppy is trying to take the nuke apart to keep it from killing us all and you're not making it any easier."

"No problem," Dalton called from the cab of the truck. "I'll slow down so the people behind us can catch up and shoot us."

Sam threw a quick look out the back of the truck to see that the bad guys had indeed caught up. Wes and the other guys were barely able to keep them at bay. Even as he watched, one of the vehicles chasing them caught up and slammed into Wes's truck, nearly shoving it off the road. And based on the view Sam got as they went around another curve, going off the road this deep in the mountains meant a drop of a couple hundred feet. As if bad guys with guns weren't enough to deal with.

Another curve had the truck tires squawking and the nuke sliding back Sam's direction. Dalton might drive them off the edge of a cliff before the bad guys ever got a chance to shoot them. Or the burning nuke blew them up.

Sam ended up alternating between helping

Poppy with the nuke and moving to the tailgate of the truck to shoot at the bad guys. Bullets tore through the back of the truck a few times, but Poppy was so focused on what she was doing, she didn't seem to notice.

She'd gotten most of the access panels off the warhead to reveal all kinds of parts that didn't mean a damn thing to him. But he could definitely see where several bullets had penetrated into the inner case of the weapon. Gray and yellow powdery material had come out and was scattered all over the place. That looked bad, but it wasn't the part of the missile Poppy seemed to care about. Instead, she was focused on a stainless-steel cylinder the size of a long beer can. The thing had a hole in the side and was glowing a dull red, as well as belching sparks, flames, and smoke. The wires, circuit cards, and epoxy all around the metal can were smoking and burning like crazy. Poppy calmly reached into her pack and pulled out a tiny red fire extinguisher then sprayed the entirety of the mess. The stainless-steel can continued to spit fire, but everything else stopped burning.

"This is much better than I thought," she said.

"What is it?" he asked, firing a long burst of automatic weapon fire at one of the vehicles that was getting way too close, then stumbling to her side as the truck slid around a curve and almost tipped over. The missile container and all the parts Poppy had removed slid, too, nearly crushing him again.

"This is a thermal battery," she said, not looking at him as she started unbolting a bracket holding the metal cylinder down.

"A thermal battery?" he prompted.

She gave him a smile. "It produces electricity by igniting a pyrotechnical material inside, which in turn melts the electrolyte material. It was hit by one of the bullets, which inadvertently started it, creating a thermal runaway scenario."

Thermal runaway sounded pretty bad to him, but he remained silent, focusing on keeping the missile from sliding around and crushing her as she removed the battery, then tossed it out the back of the truck.

"What the hell was that?" Holden shouted over the radio from behind them, their small truck swerving to avoid the smoking thing as it bounced down the road.

"It was a piece of the warhead," Sam said casually into his mic. "But don't worry. Poppy said it isn't important."

The shooting, swerving, and sliding continued as Poppy took a can of spray foam insulation out of her pack and squirted it all over the insides of the warhead. The goop started expanding, making a mess.

His confusion must have been obvious because she smiled again.

"The expanding foam will stabilize the explosives and lithium," she explained, spraying more of the gooey stuff until it was oozing all over the place. "That's the gray and yellow pieces you saw floating around in there."

Sam would have asked what the lithium was for, but before he could, something slammed into the back of the truck and he found himself lying face down on the floor, weapon who knew where, as he was nearly crushed by the nuke.

He was so focused on Poppy and making sure she was okay that he didn't realize there was trouble coming until Major Tae came hurtling over the tailgate of the truck, falling into the back of the vehicle like he'd been shot out of a cannon. The a-hole must have been riding on the hood of the vehicle that had rammed them like he was in some action movie. There was no other way he could have gotten inside with them.

Sam lunged to his feet, frantically looking for his weapon, at the same time tracking Tae before the guy had a chance to regain his balance. But the movement barely seemed to bother the big man. The North Korean soldier aimed vicious strikes to Sam's chest and throat even as they both fell. The second they slammed into the metal flooring, Tae pulled his sidearm and aimed the gun at Sam's head.

Cursing, Sam fought back, the two of them rolling around the back of the truck, bouncing off the side rails, the tailgate, and the nuke. All the while, Tae tried to get a clear shot as Sam spent his time trying to stop him.

Poppy ducked and dived, trying to stay out of the way.

Tae got off several shots, barely missing Sam, Poppy, and the nuke. Sam was finally forced to go for the man's weapon, which left him wide open to a kick in the chest. Even though Tae was off balance and couldn't get much force behind the move, the blow still hurt his battered chest like hell, making breathing seem like something that wasn't worth the effort. It also shoved him halfway across the bed of the truck, giving Tae a chance to twist his weapon around in Sam's direction again.

Even though Sam knew he was screwed, he lunged forward anyway. Because going down without a fight, wasn't an option. If he failed, Poppy would be next.

Tae hesitated for a moment, a smile stretching across his face. As if he wanted Sam to know just how much he was going to enjoy this. Then the big man lifted his weapon a little higher and started to squeeze the trigger.

Sam leaped forward even though he knew there was no way to get to Tae in time. But instead of getting a bullet for his trouble, he saw the North Korean stumble sideways as a white blur hit him in the side of the head. The man's shot went wide as a burst of powdery foam engulfed his head.

Poppy had sprayed him with her tiny fire extinguisher.

Using the distraction to his advantage, Sam finished the fight, shoving Tae out the back of the truck.

Sam almost fell out with him, but he grabbed onto the top of the tailgate at the last second. That gave him a front row seat to Major Tae hitting the road and getting run over by one of his own vehicles, which ended up sliding right off the mountainside.

That seemed to take something out of the few bad guys still trying to catch them. A couple exchanged a few more rounds with Wes's vehicle, but after that, the entire group gave up the chase. Seconds later, it was just them and one hastily patched-up nuke. The drive was almost pleasant now that they weren't being shot at.

Sam looked over as a warm hand came down to cover his where it rested on the top of the tailgate. Poppy seemed frazzled but was still holding the small fire extinguisher she'd used to save his life. Maybe he'd get the thing bronzed.

"Is it over?" Poppy asked, leaning her weight into him a little. He was sore as hell from all the fighting but having her there against him felt nice. Really nice.

"We still have to get the nuke to the beach and signal the sub for a pickup," he said softly, gazing at her and wondering how he ever got so lucky. "But yeah, I think the exciting part is over."

Poppy leaned in and kissed him. Damn, did she taste good. If he wasn't so sore—and sitting a few feet away from a damaged nuclear weapon—Sam thought he might like to see where the kiss could lead. But then Poppy pulled back, a tired smile on her face.

"Good," she said. "Because after this, I never want to go in the field again for the rest of my life. You can keep this adrenaline crap all for yourself."

A small part of him was disappointed that this would be their only adventure together like this. But then he kissed her again, thinking that it was probably for the best. He decided he didn't deal well with seeing Poppy in danger.

"Guys," Wes's voice sounded over the radio. "You know we can see you two kissing from back here, right? We'd tell you to get a room, but that isn't an option right now."

Chuckling, Sam started to pull away, but Poppy reached out and stopped him. "Let them watch," she murmured against his lips. "I don't care."

Sam decided that he didn't either.

CHAPTER
Fifteen

"So, we're doing this again?" Poppy asked, staring out the passenger side window of Sam's truck at the extremely familiar house they were parked in front of. "It seems like we were here a couple weeks ago, and that time didn't end so well."

Beside her, Sam let out a warm, soft laugh, and Poppy couldn't help but turn to look his way, her heartwarming for the dozenth time today at the sight of him.

"It seems like two weeks because it's *been* two weeks since we were here." He leaned over to kiss her gently. "Fourteen days exactly, actually. But I promise, this time, the day will end differently."

He kissed her again, making it difficult to think about anything else. Maybe she could talk him into going back to her place and spending the day making out instead of facing another Travers family cookout.

Not that she was expecting any issues at the party. Everyone who'd known the make-believe version of Poppy were now fully aware of the real her. After the mission to Indonesia, Sam's Teammates accepted her as one of their own now. But even though Sam's parents knew the truth, it didn't make facing them again any easier. She couldn't help thinking that they were never going to think she was good enough for their son.

"Come on," Sam whispered as he pulled back and opened his door. "It's going to be fine. I promise."

Poppy didn't say anything as Sam led her through his parents' house and into the backyard. The tables had been set up exactly the same, with the same tablecloths and the same dishes full of sides and desserts. Like the past two weeks had never happened and she was right back here for the first time.

Chasen and Lane were the first two people they ran into, and the conversation immediately devolved into a discussion of what had happened after the mission.

"I'm still tearing down the weapon," Poppy said. "But we're going to gain mountains of intel on where the North Koreans are with their nuclear program. What about you guys? Did you ever figure out what happened to Colonel Kam and Abyasa Alatas?"

Chasen frowned. "Unfortunately, we have no idea where either of them are. Lucero has confirmed that Kam never went back to North Korea, not that anyone expected him to. Beyond that, we don't know if Kam and Alatas killed each other or went into hiding."

Their conversation was halted when Sam's sister, Madison ran up to hug Poppy. "I made a ninety-eight on my calculus test," she said with a grin. "Highest in the class!"

At fifteen, Madison was Sam's youngest sibling. He'd brought her over to Poppy's apartment a few days ago to get some help with her math homework, and the two of them had bonded over double integration techniques. It turned out that Madison was a math nerd, and after finding out that Poppy was a math savant, the younger girl pretty much thought she hung the moon.

Sam smiled as Poppy and his little sister stood there in the middle of the yard getting excited over test results. Poppy loved helping Madison with math, but even more, she loved seeing Sam smile.

Madison took her around to meet everyone at the cookout she hadn't met before, even though Poppy insisted that wasn't necessary. Though truthfully, it helped having the girl around for some of the introductions. Like Dalton's wife, Kimber, and his little girl, Emma. Everyone had decided that Poppy and Dalton dating was classified beyond belief, but she still felt a little uncomfortable meeting his family, even if Kimber was as sweet as all get out and Emma was completely adorable.

Poppy didn't relax until she'd made a complete circuit of the party and talked to everyone—including Sam's parents. This time around, Melissa surprised her by hugging her.

"Kurt told me that you saved Sam's life on that mission you went on with him," she said softly in Poppy's ear. "Thank you."

She and Sam chatted with his parents for a

while, talking about the classes Poppy was teaching this semester and what movies they'd been watching on Netflix.

"So, when are you two moving in together?" Melissa asked casually, looking back and forth from Poppy to Sam. At the stunned look they gave her, she added, "Madison mentioned you still haven't unpacked any boxes, Sam, so it wasn't hard to figure out you haven't been sleeping there."

Poppy exchanged looks with Sam, who simply grinned.

"We've talked about moving in together, but figured maybe we should take our time," Poppy said.

"Yeah," Sam added. "No reason to do something that might put added stress on our relationship. We can see where things stand in a few months, when Poppy has to renew the lease on her apartment."

It was Melissa and Kurt's turn to exchange looks.

"That's a very smart decision," Melissa said, her lips curving into a knowing smile.

Sam's parents wandered off a little while after

that, but only after she and Sam promised they'd come over for dinner the following weekend.

Poppy let out the breath she didn't know she'd been holding. "That went better than I thought it would."

"I have no idea what you were worried about," Sam said with a chuckle as he kissed her. "I told you my parents would love you."

Poppy smiled up at him. "Speaking of love, have I mentioned lately that I love you?"

"As a matter of fact, you told me this morning," he said with a grin. "Somewhere in between your second orgasm and me professing my undying love for you. But feel free to say you love me as often as you like. I'll never get tired of hearing it."

She laughed. She'd never imagined falling in love so quickly, but like Sam, she was never going to get tired of hearing those three little words either.

It was later, as she and Sam were sitting around with everyone that Poppy realized what being with Sam truly meant. She had an entire group of amazing friends as well as an even more amazing boyfriend. After going on that Indonesian mission and knowing how dangerous Sam's job really was, she couldn't help but think that having people like this around when he had to run off to save the world was going to be more important than she'd realized.

"You okay?" he asked softly.

Poppy supposed she'd zoned out there for a bit, thinking about what life with Sam was going to be like.

"Yes," she said, leaning over to kiss him. "I'm definitely okay."

For more Military Heroes check out my SWAT, STAT, and X-OPS Series!

SWAT: Special Wolf Alpha Team

Hungry Like the Wolf

Wolf Trouble

In the Company of Wolves

To Love a Wolf

Wolf Unleashed

Wolf Hunt

Wolf Hunger

Wolf Rising

Wolf Rebel

Wolf Untamed

Rogue Wolf

paigetylertheauthor.com/books/#wolf

STAT: Special Threat Assessment Team

Wolf Under Fire

Undercover Wolf

True Wolf

paigetylertheauthor.com/books/#stat

X-OPS

Her Perfect Mate

Her Lone Wolf

Her Wild Hero

Her Fierce Warrior

Her Rogue Alpha

Her True Match

Her Dark Half

Exposed

paigetylertheauthor.com/books/#ops

Looking for Romantic Comedy?

Then check out The "IT" Girls Series!
The "IT" Girls
Kali & Grayson
Sutton & Boone
Liv & Cash
paigetylertheauthor.com/books/#itgirls

ABOUT PAIGE

Paige Tyler is a *New York Times* and *USA Today* Bestselling Author of sexy, romantic suspense and paranormal romance. She and her very own military hero (also known as her husband) live on the beautiful Florida coast with their adorable fur baby (also known as their dog). Paige graduated with a degree in education, but decided to pursue her passion and write books about hunky alpha males and the kick-butt heroines who fall in love with them.

www.paigetylertheauthor.com

To be notified about Paige's new releases, get exclusive sneak peeks at upcoming books, deleted scenes, exclusive short stories, and giveaways, sign up for her newsletter. Your email will never be shared with anyone.

Sign Me Up!

paigetylertheauthor.com/subscribe

I'm excited to announce that I now have a FAN group on FB! It's a place to hang out with other fans—and me! Share stories and pictures, discuss what you love about my X-OPS, SWAT, Dallas Fire & Rescue, and SEALs of Coronado Series, as well as my other books!

And best of all, get sneak peeks before anyone else!

Hope to see you there!

www.facebook.com/groups/Paigetylersgroupies

CPSIA information can be obtained
at www.ICGtesting.com
Printed in the USA
LVHW021636051021
699597LV00007B/914

9 798201 593063